700 Gentlemen

Dead West, Volume 1

Elijah Cooksey

Published by Elijah Cooksey, 2018.

This is a work of fiction. Similarities to real people, places, or events are entirely coincidental.

700 GENTLEMEN

First edition. April 7, 2018.

Written by Elijah Cooksey.

Ron Davidson

Not the John Wayne you would had liked,

but close.

700

THE SUN HAD WORN ON the bare country, exhausting it to a worthless state. Ankle-high bee bush and barberry were scattered amongst the sloped landscape. You could see the air near the ground steaming up till it didn't anymore. A man wearing a weathered overcoat walked alone. The crown of his Stetson reached past his nose, covering the better part of his face. His boots ground loose dirt and sand against the clay earth. Sweat collected at the curve of his jaw then drizzled down from there. The sound of small metal pieces being tossed about scraped with every step the man made. The sound came from the pockets of his suit jacket, which were vast enough to fit hundreds of coins, or other noisy, pocket-sized objects. But this man didn't look like the type to have that kind of currency. Instead, he looked like he was carrying something malicious, and he walked on, clattering, toward a lonely church about a mile out.

The mission ahead was a passable shack made of adobe. Aesthetics weren't a concern of the Spanish settlers who had traversed through the exhausting land when they had built it, and compared to the grandness of the missions built along the western coast, it was unmemorable. Simple benches lined the single-roomed church and a dull cast-iron bell hung over the heads of the congregation. The altar sat vacant with a simple wooden podium placed at its side, but thirty or more were seated amongst the pews chatting to spend the time before service.

1

A few children gathered at a particular corner marveling at the chalice of holy water and the decorative canteen that sat beside it, but were promptly shooed away by a priest. Tired of seeing the usual routine every Sunday, Jesse would wait outside until the bell called him in.

Despite being in his forties, Jesse had soft, hairless skin and an immature bone structure. No one, save for Jesse himself, would disagree if he was called a "baby face." He dressed as young as he looked, wearing plain jeans and a sweat-stained shirt as if the only reason he had clothes on was because of their necessity. He was arguing with his father some distance from the entrance, almost out of earshot of the church regulars making their way through the mission portal. The two began shouting, which prompted Maryanne, the church patriarch, to grimace. Jesse's father noticed, so he went inside leaving Jesse around the corner of the mission.

Jesse drank from his flask, but spit up from the warmth at first. He finished the rest of the whiskey, which stung his weathered lips, then traced over the country uneasily, until his eye caught on a lone man approaching from the east. Jesse thought it was odd that the man was walking through untrailed territory. Nothing was out in that direction that was manageable on foot, and even on horseback one would need a heaping of water and trail supplies. Fact was, the nearest town to the east was Delamar, and Jesse and his father had deserted it along with the rest of its inhabitants years ago. If that man had come from that way without any food and water, he would be head down in the sand baking soon enough. Jesse marched into the church past his father, who was sitting in the third row of pews, and they both made a good business of not looking at each other. Jesse grabbed an empty canteen that was hanging by a nail in the wall near the podium and took it outside and filled it with the water from the barrel placed by the hitching rail. When he came back around the mission corner, he couldn't spot the man anymore. He waited for a few minutes, then poured out the canteen letting the water cut through the sand and stream along the clay.

When a hand bell rang, Jesse crept into the service and sat at an empty pew near the back, a few aisles behind his pa. The congregation fell silent and began to pray. Jesse waited for the rest of the church before bowing his head and falling to his knees. He liked being last. Before his eyes shut, a clinking sound distracted him, and he turned to the church door. The man that Jesse had seen out in the desert stood there in the opening. The crown of the man's hat grazed the archway as he stepped through. Uneasy about the metal clattering the man made with each step, Jesse didn't look away as the man paced the walkway between the rows of aisle.

The man walked up past each pew and climbed those few steps at the altar, then made his way behind the small wooden podium as if to address the church like a priest. The man removed his hat, revealing a mangled horror. Scars, blade-thin, distorted the symmetry of his face. The bottom of his lip was burnt black, with parts of the top permanently swollen and crusted. He had a dead eye, which was cocked looking out to his left. His ears had been chewed; one was completely gone, while the other was a hanging flab of skin.

When the man spoke, the church strained to understand his broken speech.

"Delamar," the man shouted. Jesse glanced at the exit and scooted closer. "Who is from Delamar?" The man tried again as he shifted his fingers within his pocket. A few people raised their hands cautiously, Jesse's father being one of them. The man was displeased. "Who else." Behind the podium, the man positioned the barrel of an Iver Johnson revolver toward the church. Fourteen hands were raised, thirteen of them males—the last, Maryanne. Jesse's hand shook in his lap until he begrudgingly lifted it to shoulder-level.

The hammer of the Iver Johnson cocked into place. When the man pulled the trigger, the bullet broke through the wooden face of the podium and hit the cast-iron bell above. The bell rang with a force that could shatter eardrums. Everyone covered their ears and shut their eyes as if dynamite had been set off at their feet. The man, unbothered by the shrieking cast-iron bell, lifted the five-cylinder pocket gun and unloaded the remaining four chambers in queue behind the first. The revolver fired like a child's cap gun, making low popping noises instead of thunderous bangs, lacking a noticeable recoil. Each bullet entered the skull of a person who had had their hand raised, a person who had lived in Delamar.

The man unlocked the hinge with his thumb and slung the top break open with a sharp flick, letting the empty casings fall behind the podium and revealing the empty cylinders. He then slid the open gun into his pocket and shook it about, shuffling the loose bullets until five snugged into their respective chamber. The barrel was still steaming when he had it loaded and snapped back together, and then he emptied the chambers as swiftly as he had loaded them into five other poor souls. They crashed to the ground motionless. One of them was Jesse's father, and for a moment Jesse thought his dad might turn around and say "I'm alright," but his father didn't move. The man stepped forward past the altar and let his casings clatter to the floor there as he reloaded.

The bell's vibration finally died. Jesse stumbled toward the exit as the church scattered like mice being unearthed from floorboards. He sprinted around the corner of the mission and another volley of shots burst out. The rounds fired so closely together their low pops merged into one. People scurried out from the mission portal, though they were a good deal behind Jesse, who had already covered about fifteen yards and was franticly sprinting.

Jesse's tears mixed with his sweat. "I ought to had done something."

The man paced to the doorway and spotted Jesse fleeing out to the country. With the distance that stood between them, a seasoned marksman would have trouble even with a rifle shot. The man trained the almost paper-thin sights on Jesse, which was much like aiming at a hare fifty yards out, and fired. The bullet cut through Jesse's calf, sending him to a knee. Sand grinded against his kneecap, ripping holes in his pants, and his blood colored the barren earth. The man watched him lie out face-down in the sand before deciding Jesse was a dead man, and then he turned back toward the church. When Jesse saw this, he cursed as he rose and started away, hobbling madly and sucking at air as he did. Hot blood poured from his calf, drenching his pant leg as he pressed on.

"Don't you quit," Jesse ordered himself. The spinning desert disorientated him. He focused on a bee bush ahead, using it to guide him in one direction, despite the feeling of vertigo that had come over him. His boot sloshed with each step, blood spilling out the shaft. "Don't you lay down and die, damn it." He stumbled over himself, then collapsed into the earth, fainting there in the wilderness. A red trail of blood traced his path back to the mission's acre.

Before the man returned to the service hall, Maryanne had hidden herself behind the podium and waited for what seemed like hours. She covered her mouth and peeked through the bullet hole that revolver had left. Airborne particles of wood irritated her already wet, red eyes as she peered through.

The man stepped over the bodies thrown astray amongst the pews. One body twitched, his leg splashing up excess blood from the pool at his feet. Maryanne couldn't look away as this mad man inspected the faces of the dead. He would lean close to examine the lifelessness until he was satisfied, then continue to the nearest body, flipping them face-up if he had to. Maryanne moved her head back slightly to rub her eye, but clipped the side of the podium as she did. She froze, listening. The man's head whipped toward the podium. Jingle. Jingle. Jingle. He grasped the podium and threw it aside, uncovering Maryanne.

"Higgans," the man grunted. Maryanne gaped at the figure before her. When the man spoke, she saw the inside of his deformed mouth. Few teeth had survived, and those that did were out of place and looked like they could be yanked out with the strength of a forefinger. His gums were rigid and viscous, with portions boiled out.

"Where are they?" The man aimed his gun at her bosom.

Maryanne's lips quivered before muttering "Aqua Dulce." The man looked at her till she continued, "California, near the Vazquez Rocks."

"Vazquez." The man paced to the saucer of holy water.

As he did, Maryanne shouted, "Why!"

"Oh, you know why, Maryanne. You're well aware of the Devil's crimes that were done in Delamar. Those men will pay their debt."

Maryanne scrambled to her feet and hurried out, stumbling over the bodies and shrieking as she did. The man fitted his hands around the chalice's underside and lifted the edge of the saucer to his lips, drinking the holy water dry.

―――――――――

THE WAGON ROAD WAS littered with potholes and rocks that bucked Samuel O'Hara on and off his seat and made the windshield rattle. The black automobile was like a furnace. O'Hara could feel the heat on his skin. His fingers gripped the curve of the steering wheel while he watched the path ahead.

He had two more years before he turned thirty, and he considered himself a man who had spent his spry years. Beneath the gorge of his suit jacket, pinned to his undershirt, was a U.S. Marshal badge.

It wasn't long till O'Hara reached the mission. A crowd had gathered outside. Two other Model Ts were parked only feet from the hitching rail. O'Hara noticed the blood splatters on the mission walls had already morphed from pale red to a dried brown.

When O'Hara stepped inside, his face soured from the decayed stench.

"Ain't smelling too pretty," a Sheriff called with his back to the Marshal.

"It's not a looker either," O'Hara added. Sheriff Reed jolted at the voice of the stranger. At first, Reed thought someone from the crowd had grown curious and poked in. That thought was dismissed when he got a look at O'Hara and the badge pinned at his chest.

"Now what could be bothering you, Marshal? I can't reckon that this is your matter," Reed asked.

O'Hara heard the question, but paused. His mind was already busy with the scene. He scanned the pews, counting the bodies as he did. He found all thirteen, despite a few being hidden behind toppled pews and buried under piles.

"I'm poking around, wondering if that's alright, Sheriff."

"You're the Marshal."

"If I didn't have a badge, reckon I'd be shooed out the door."

"Lots of, curious cats, and too often they leave a mess. Or spread it around," Reed waggled his fingers about when he said this.

O'Hara nodded, "Those cats just see it as the next good read in the paper, not the damn tragedy it is."

"Well, it ought to make a man wake at night," The Sheriff said as he held his hand out to the Marshal. The two introduced themselves with a sturdy handshake, and Reed told the Marshal that any help he could offer was more than welcome. Then the two went about the scene in their own particular way.

Reed prodded the bodies carefully. He counted bullet wounds and compared the placement of the shots. All were above the neck or at the heart. O'Hara paced through the pews swiftly, checking each body for certain details at a glance. He made his way to the podium, which was still tipped on its side, and brought it upright and sat it where he figured it had originally been. Reed had just crouched over a third body when the Marshal finished his work.

"Someone got away," O'Hara stated.

"Sure. Most the church did," Reed said with a touch of condescension.

"Most the church kept their lives because they were allowed to. But one man, he escaped."

Reed glanced at the room, trying to find what had given the Marshal that opinion.

"We have thirteen bodies, all with one bullet in em. Whoever did this knew his gun. Each shot is in the head or near the heart. And he shot from the podium. See that bullet hole in the wood face? This hole ain't large, and the wood is splintered out toward the church," O'Hara continued as he outlined the tunneled wood with his finger. "And he walked up to the altar before anyone bolted, because every shot can be lined up with this point here and, if you look at how these casings are here together, seems like a rough group of five behind the podium and another in front. Let's say he used a five-cartridge revolver. It's small enough to hide, so he could have positioned himself. And it fits with the hole in the podium and the shells." O'Hara paused before continuing, imagining the Sheriff might have an objection. "This hole is aimed at the bell. Yup, there is where the bullet got it." O'Hara pointed at the streaked, indented mark the bullet had left on the bell. "How's your arithmetic, Sheriff?"

"Thirteen bodies and one bullet in that fine bell. With a five-cartridge revolver, we ought to be looking for a shot." O'Hara nodded before Reed went on. "I've been counting rounds since I could hold a gun. But it's possible he only wanted to kill thirteen men. The numbers don't work as often as you'd think or like em to."

O'Hara agreed to the possibility, suggesting they ride up a couple hundred yards from the mission to confirm one idea or the other.

They found the blood stains fifty yards out. It was an easy trail to make out; the dried blood was prominent against the clay earth. After they followed the stained sand for a mile farther, its trace became sparse. Reed suggested that coyotes could have made off with the corpse, and neither thought there was any worth in a prolonged search. When they returned to the church, Reed's partner Earl was waiting for them with a witness, Maryanne, who introduced herself to the Marshal.

"Maryanne, was it? Please, if you'd kindly. I'd like to ask you some questions around the corner here," O'Hara began, being as delicate as he could.

She nodded, and O'Hara gestured for her to walk ahead of him. She did, but slowly, as if her feet were too heavy for her. She had to be wearing the same dress, the Marshal realized, noting the blood stains. It had been a couple hours since the incident, and from what O'Hara assumed, she had fled the scene and only now returned to offer her testimony. So she had been home, or wherever she was between the killings and now, for the better part of eight hours. It was enough time to change—plenty of time.

When they made it around the corner, O'Hara asked, "So how bout you tell me about yourself. You got a husband?"

"No."

"Are you widowed?"

"Yes. Marshal, I don't understand where this is leading," she whispered sharply.

"Details are important, ma'am. That's all I'm getting on about."

Maryanne turned her face away and watched the country out in front of her. Her fingers fidgeted, scrubbing against each other. The arm sleeves of her dress stopped above her wrist, and the fabric had red stains that led up to her elbows. O'Hara thought the forearm stains were a good deal brighter than the others on the dress. They seemed more recent. She broke the silence, "Alright, get on about it. But I have something important to tell you."

O'Hara made eye contact and brought his hand to hers and gave it a firm squeeze. "Things will be alright. Try to calm down for me if you can." He had pressed his thumb onto the sleeve of the dress nearest her hand; it felt damp. Without giving it any more thought he asked, "So what have you been doing since you left the church and now?"

Maryanne looked at the Marshal out of the side of her eye. "I drove home, fast as I could."

"What did you do then?"

"When I was home?"

"Yes."

"Marshal, I have something I need to—"

"Answer my question, ma'am."

Her lips quivered, then she cried. "I got home and I did this," she emphasized her tears by fanning her flushed cheeks. "I cried! And prayed!"

O'Hara stood there as she sobbed and let her calm down before he concluded, "Thanks for your time, ma'am."

"No, that isn't it," Maryanne persisted.

"Look here, I ain't getting the info I ought to be getting. Maybe it'd be best if you and the Sheriff spoke in a couple of nights."

"He is out to do this again! He is heading toward Aqua Dulce, and he will massacre the Higgans' ranch."

The Marshal leaned forward and lowered his voice to a stern hush. "You wouldn't be fibbing to a Law Marshal, now would you, ma'am?"

"I swear it."

Marshal O'Hara asked Maryanne to wait in the mission's field before returning to Reed and his partner inside.

"All men, eh," Earl stated with an impish grin. "Thinking the killer has a loony vendetta against men?" He chuckled. "I know who it was."

"That right?" Reed played along.

"Yup. Damn ex-wife was serious this time."

The two turned to O'Hara when they noticed him walking in. "Do me a favor would ya, Sheriff?" O'Hara asked.

"Go ahead."

"That Maryanne, she's all pale face right now. Could you question her again in a couple days or so? She ain't saying something that ought to be said, keeping something to herself that we ought to know."

"Yeah that ain't a problem, Marshal. You mind if I ask why you want me doing this?" Reed inquired in a genuine manner. "Seems like you would do more good."

"I'm heading to Aqua Ducle in the morning. She said that's where our man-at-large will be, so I better be there too."

"You sure you are fit chasing this crazed steer without any other guns?" Earl asked.

"You two don't have authority out of the state. Reed would be good company, but that ain't on the table. And I don't carry a gun."

"Are you a damned loon?"

"Never needed one before."

"It often takes me a while to tell the intelligence of a man," the Sheriff interjected. "Earl, I could tell right away how quick Marshal O'Hara is. One of the smartest men I met, and I only known him for an afternoon, He ain't a fool. But, Marshal, you are chasing something you haven't before. It is high time you pick up a holster and a good piece to fill it," the Sheriff urged.

"I'll give it a night."

"I'll write to you bout what Maryanne has to say, and Earl believes it's best if we go out the country further looking for our missing bullet. I'll let you know if it turns up."

The Marshal thanked Reed and agreed that anything that the sheriff had to write about the case would be helpful, believing that he would be hearing about Maryanne soon enough.

O'Hara parted from the investigators and began his ride back along the uneven path. He pulled to the side when the church was out of sight, and just sat there and thought. It has been an eventful time ever since he took up the Marshal badge four years ago. He had seen plenty of death, most from Indian land disputes or Mexican drug running. This felt different though, and he couldn't figure why it did. He looked down at his hip—it never felt empty like this before.

IT WAS A BARREN CHAMBER buried underneath the earth six feet down like a grave, and it smelled like one too. It was the stench of rot that wiggles in your throat and makes you gag. A winding staircase led to a one-man cell that hadn't been used since the eighteen-hundreds. Back yonder when it had been dug up and the walls layered with brick and adobe, the idea was to have a hush spot to lodge any person with an approach different from the popular opinion.

The man who had paid for this work went by the name of Grand. He had gotten his use out of the prison by keeping the space occupied permanently. This policy had had a greater influence over the duration a man had to stay in the cell compared to the severity of his crime. Usually, a man was trapped until it was time for someone else. One town local had been jailed for the better part of the cold season for firing his revolver during Sunday service, while Timothy Singer, the boy who had been caught foolin' with the minister's daughter, didn't leave till she was married and moved on to Texas. Fact, for every day the cell set empty, it had further pressured Grand to search for an occupant. There was one point where he had locked his own son there, but that was short-lived thanks to the way Timothy spent his free time. Before Grand had died, he had sold the manor, complete with the basement cell, to a Captain who had sailed to the States with a crew that had been contracted for the benefit of the Queen. Truth was, the Captain had told Grand upon purchase of the cell that he and his crew had a similar practice aboard the Queen's vessel. Grand had then become confident that the cell would continue to have its use with the Captain.

Daniel was in that cell now and he had stayed in that cell for four years and a little change. During those years it wasn't all too eventful. On an average day, Daniel just lay on his side and counted the water drops collecting on the floor. There wasn't any means to relieve himself, so he had a corner of the cell dedicated to that sort of business. When the smell got so bad that it seeped up the stairway into the living space, a house hand would come down with a bucket of boiled water and a broom and then went about dealing with it. Daniel grew accustomed to the smell, but on those days when the hot water kicked it back up in the air, he had to breathe into his shirt. A lot of men would have gagged and probably vomited, but Daniel didn't have that option on account of not having any substance in his stomach.

Other than seeing the house hand, whose frequency depended on Daniel's diet, he never really saw anyone else, other than Margot, who had come down to the cell on three occasions.

The first time Margot came was only a few days after Daniel had been put up in that cell. Then he was young and still looked like a healthy boy who was not only presentable, but if he was your kid, chance was the whole town would be hearing you go on about what a handsome and learned boy you got. Oh, his mother used to brag alright, and his late father would have bragged, if his lungs hadn't quit on him.

Margot had come down the stairway carefully, keeping the bowl of homemade soup steady in her palms.

"Mrs. Margot," Daniel pleaded, approaching as close as the cell bars allowed. "The Captain was an animal. I didn't have no choice to what I did. And what the Captain said, it ain't all that happened."

Margot nearly dropped the bowl in shock.

"See, Margot, I didn't do it. You gotta let me go."

Margot stepped close to the cell before hissing, "Is that right?"

Daniel stammered back. He had to realign himself before continuing on. "Yeah, that's right."

"If that's right, then who is wrong?" Margot asked.

"What do ya mean who is wrong?"

"You saying the Captain is wrong?"

"In a way, yes, ma'am."

Margot let the bowl fall from her hands and it shattered at the foot of the cell where the soup pooled out. "Don't you bad mouth the Captain, boy."

"It's true. I swear it, ma'am."

"Liar!" Margot cursed.

She left and no one came down to give Daniel anything to eat for three days. After the soup had hardened at the base of the cell bars for a day, Daniel licked up most of what he could.

It was a long while till Margot came down to the cell again, and Daniel was not happy to see her when she did. It had been months of being fed rotten food, and he was weak and boney from it. She had something heavy behind her back, but Daniel, starved as he was, only cared about the loaf of bread she was holding out in front of her chest. Daniel crawled to the cell bars and reached out, but Margot slapped his hands away.

"Take a bite through the bars," she instructed.

Daniel struggled to get the thick of his head through the opening between the bars, but when he did, his head snugged in roughly. He tried to take a bite from the loaf when Margot held it out close to him, but something had forced his head to the floor, slamming his jaw against the brick, and causing him to sink his teeth into a chunk of his tongue. Margot had taken a plank of wood and pinned the back of Daniel's neck with it so he hit the floor. Then Margot tied the plank there, trapping Daniel's head. He didn't have the strength to fight it, and his experience had already shown him that hollering was no use. Blood seeped over his bottom lip when he looked up at Margot.

"Next week, the town is gonna gather, and all the gentlemen of the town are gonna vote on what it is that will be done with you. Now, you are gonna be set up in front of all those gentlemen when they do the voting, and I need you to promise that the lying nature you have won't be causing no trouble." When Margot finished, Daniel made muffled sounds in response so she leaned closer to hear and when she did, Daniel spat blood on her face.

Margot came back down the stairs after that with a cattle whip in hand and went off on Daniel's face, which was still pinned between the bars. When flaps of skin started to hang over his eyes, Daniel found the strength to holler about it. When she was finally done and satisfied, Daniel wasn't able to see clearly because of the bloody lumps that had squeezed over his brow. It was a couple minutes before Margot spoke again, and when she did she told Daniel to drink. He tried to spit up all the blood from his mouth, then let his mouth hang open for Margot to put the cup to his flayed lips.

Burning pain. The inside of his mouth was melting as Margot poured a cup of boiling water into it. His mouth never quite worked after that. It took him about a year before he was able to say simple words, and even then you had to strain to understand it.

The last time Daniel saw Margot was a day after the voting had taken place and her appearance was all to say one thing to Daniel.

"I don't feel sorry for you, not one bit. Those 700 gentlemen voted you guilty, and now you are gonna hang for your sin. It's a shame I couldn't vote with them." And then she left.

Most days, though, Daniel was alone in his morbid home. The water dripped rhythmically. The drops felt like the pounds of a drum to Daniel, overtaking his thoughts completely. With each beat, hate caused his heart to boil over further. Each drop reminded him of those faces. The gentlemen of the town who had put him there to die. Those gentlemen he had never wronged who had damned him so cruelly. He counted every drop with malice. He kept track, fantasizing about the death of the gentlemen who walked six feet above him. Daniel wished to claw up from the grave and pull them beneath the dirt so they could share this hell. "They all had the power to help," he swore. "They have a debt. Joseph Raphael De Lamar," Daniel cursed. Drop. Drop. Daniel counted each drop, till 700.

687

AS THE DAY LEFT, TWILIGHT set in on the high desert and it was a relief. The rock was still hot from the long day of sun, but gusts came around the San Gabriel range carrying cooler air with it. The man swayed from the powerful mountain wind. He held onto his hat before the wind could take it on its way to the Mojave as he hiked up the face of a rock that tilted toward the mountains. There were dozens of large, flat-faced, sedimentary rocks that stretched out at about a sixty-degree angle to the open sky. The geological formations were distinguishable enough to be named after the bandit, Tiburcio Vasquez, who had used their slopes and ridges to outrun Sheriffs and the like. You can go to the rocks today; they are still named after that thieving son of a bitch, Vasquez.

The Higgans' ranch was a three-part farmhouse with a barn tucked twenty yards back. Between the barn and the farmhouse were crops of potatoes and cabbage that had been lined off with the back house. A few scrawny pigs were fenced next to the vegetables. The man navigated through an infestation of bear grass before he reached the ranch, and by that time the twilight had faded into night.

The wind began to roar and its gusts rattled the house's frame. Charles Higgans barked at his adult son to stoke the fire, then sunk his portly body into the rocker, letting himself sway back and forth lightly as he chugged from an unlabeled bottle of whiskey. Charles had the gruff look of a poor man who had lived an unlucky life, which complemented the permanent calluses on his hands. When he raised the bottle again, his hands shook despite his effort to steady them, and eventually the shaking got bad enough that the bottle crashed to the floor. His son was ordered to clean up. It was a sizable family: fifteen men and four women resided at the ranch with Charles, who was either a father or uncle depending on who it was that was asked.

His son gathered the shards of glass into a pile and dried the spilt liquor with a torn shirt. He took the shirt and glass pile to the kitchen and threw them into a trash bucket. The kitchen counter was cluttered with empty whiskey bottles which rattled about when the wind picked up, along with the flimsy backdoor which was a firm push away from breaking off its hinges. Charles grimaced when he heard another crash, the sound of shattering preceded by a light pop in the wind.

Charles exclaimed, "Damn, boy, we ain't marrying no Jews! Keep away from them glass! Christ help me." Charles shut his eyes and leaned farther back. After about five minutes he got a feeling someone was above him looking down.

The barrel of the revolver was still warm from its last shot; Charles felt the heated steel on his forehead.

"D-Daniel," Charles stammered. The man stared down the sights with an eerie stillness. "You should have a seat, I'll grab you a glass," Charles continued.

"I ain't gonna sit."

"Look, I knew they was doing some wrong thing, you know. That is why I got my family here, and see we got ourselves moved on," Charles reasoned.

The man's forefinger caressed the bottom of the cylinder before stopping to greet the trigger.

"I'm sorry! We all real sorry," Charles begged.

"You ain't sorry for what you did, you sorry for what's coming." Daniel bored the revolver into Charles's forehead and his wrinkled skin folded over the circumference of the barrel. "I'm sure Higgans and all you gentlemen from Delamar sorry now."

"Please, I—" The revolver popped, speaking over Charles.

Bare branches rattled against the window pane. Sand tore off into the tempest-like gusts. The outside of the house moved, but Daniel was waiting with his revolver in hand for anyone within the house to stir, expecting that his gunfire was heard. The walls were painted brown, but tinged into an off-yellow because of the family's excessive smoking. A pungent, medicated smell drifted through the house. Daniel couldn't name the scent. He paced softly toward its source as the .32 caliber bullets shifted in his coat pockets, scratching and grinding against one another.

Daniel stopped at a door in the middle of a hallway. The chemical smell seeped through the door's crevices. He twisted the knob and eased the door open with the nose of the revolver. Smoke leaked out of the widening gap. The room wasn't furnished, just carpet and wall. Broken glass and opium pipes littered the stained carpet. One of the Higgans men was lying over his younger cousin, pinning her there on the carpet.

Daniel had never imagined he would enjoy shooting a man in the back as much as he did right then. He had always gotten a thin pleasure from the stupefied face that stared back when he shot a man. He liked seeing the power leave them. But Daniel didn't want to see this person's face; it wasn't worth looking at. So Daniel shot the back of the Higgans head out, and if Daniel was to see him in Hell, he'd shoot him in the back again and send him lower.

She didn't respond to her cousin's death, or the innards that soaked the carpet beside her. Daniel towed her limp body to the corner and covered her with a sheet and just left her there. Her glassy eyes watched Daniel close the door behind him.

Art shifted in the dark toward the main house. Sand scattered up with the current as he shielded his face with his forearm. He was the smartest of the Higgans family, though that didn't hold much merit. Years back, he had navigated the family to Aqua Dulce from Delamar—this was before the town had lost its mining reputation. Art had planned on speaking to his father about the cabbage that was being nipped up by the hares, but when he reached the kitchen window his stomach curled at the sight of his older brother. Blood had collected over the tile and curved around shards of glass. Art stood there in the roaring wind for a minute before he bolted back to the adjacent farmhouse where he woke the six other Higgans boys and told them what he had seen. Then the sky lit up with the glow of red flame, and warmth overtook the night air.

"Hell, the barn!" one shouted. A fire rose past the roof of the barn and illuminated the farm land around it. Wind fed the flame at a mad rate creating a wild blaze. The men rushed toward the doomed barn and were joined by the other five Higgans boys who had noticed the fire as well. Art grabbed the shotgun from the cabinet and a couple boxes of shells, then followed his brothers and cousins at a good distance back, loading the shotgun as he did. Each of the shotgun shells had an "H" engraved into the brass.

Art stalked forward slowly, keeping his mouth slightly ajar. He concentrated on the sounds around him. The currents whipped up the blaze, his family shouted while their boots stampeded through the tough land, and then he heard a pop. Another followed immediately. He fell to the clay ground and covered his head. He waited, listening. One brother shrieked in pain, another cried out he'd been shot, then a flurry of pops burst out. Art tilted his head up. The fire was blinding, but he could partly make out the silhouettes of his family lying out in the farm land. After another volley of shots had rung out, Art was confident of the source and when he had crawled about fifteen yards west, he knew the killer was nearby. He panned over the shadowy rows of crops, searching for the gunman the same way he normally scanned for hares, but it was too dark for Art to see because his eyes had not yet adjusted from the firelight.

When another round of shots burst out Art tucked his head and covered his ears. Art judged he must be close enough to reach out and touch the intruder's leg, so he pointed the shotgun toward the noise and pulled the trigger.

Daniel grunted and fell back. A second case of pellets splintered into the clay and the soil it kicked up showered onto the brim of Daniel's Stetson. He directed his revolver and shot back into the dark. Boots shuffled away frantically. After refilling the chambers of his piece, Daniel scooted nearer to Art as he backpedaled toward the main house.

Art thought he had killed the man, and when a shot was returned, he figured there had to have been two of them. That would explain the rapid firing, he supposed. Just as Art finished loading the shotgun, a bullet ripped through his lower side. His shirt was immediately soaked through as blood trailed down his trousers. He limped away, firing the pellet shot blindly. The force from the shotgun knocked Art from his feet and he collided against the side of the main house. He propped his back up to the wall and loaded the shotgun with one arm while his left held his side which was gushing forth. Art sucked at the smoky air and started sweating from the pain. The shotgun shook in his hand as he set to raise its nose from the clay.

Daniel sat his boot atop the barrel of the shotgun, pinning it to the ground. Art pulled at the stock, but couldn't get it out from Daniel's foot. He gripped the gun with both hands, letting the pressure off his wound, and tugged with his weight to try to free the barrel. It didn't move.

"I'll kill you, like I did your fellow."

"What fellow?" Daniel muttered.

"The one you came with. I got him out there in the cabbage. He's rotting."

"My only fellow, is the devil." Daniel said before shooting Art in the core of his chest.

Daniel limped to the east, towards Vasquez Rocks, with the wind at his back. His knee was a bloody mess; several pellets had buried into the skin at the thick of the kneecap. When he made it to the flat face of a rock, he stopped and tried to pry the fragments from his leg. His fingers were too stubby to get the pebble-like pieces out, so he lifted his wounded kneecap to his mouth and used his teeth to pinch the pellets out from his leg. He wouldn't be able to get on till the next day, but he knew he was safe where he lay. Vasquez Rocks had a history of sheltering the damned.

"YOU ARE FIXING TO GET yourself killed," Stella stated with a tinge of annoyance. Her curls bounced with a gestured shake of her head. "Sammy, this isn't yours," she continued.

"Stella, it ain't about what's mine or not," Samuel broke in. "This is over Sheriff Reed's head. Something my mother said when I was young, was that if God puts a problem in your life, it's because God needs you to solve it."

Stella gripped the scruff of his coat. "Your late mother ain't looking for no favors, and God has got a lot of helpers. You're a Marshal, and my husband now, not a ride-off-into-the-night-hero, chasing after some deranged killer. We got a family coming."

"And if that man keeps walking, there are a lot of families that are going."

Stella shifted away from Samuel. "You're fixing to kill yourself. It's clear. It won't be all bad on my own, I guess."

Samuel slung his bag over his shoulder and looked out to his car parked out in the dirt. "If I ain't meant to come back, I'm sure you'll want those words back."

"I know this isn't going to ring out. I know it, Sammy. He gunned that church down like the devil asked him to. Can't imagine he will have issue with making me a lawman's widow."

Samuel turned Stella to face him directly, and when he saw her lips trembling he kissed her and got in his Model T and shut the door. She called through the window, "Buy a damned gun for my sake!"

"You know where that conversation ends."

When the car engine fired, Stella called again, "I love you, Sammy. And I would love you even if you stayed here, and I'd love your grave out there in the desert if I had to."

"I'm only worried about you loving me when I come back."

Stella watched the car roll away till O'Hara waved his hand out the window, knowing she would see it.

IT WAS A LITTLE PAST noon when O'Hara hiked past the bear grass to the front of the ranch. He paced the perimeter of the farm, counting the bodies mechanically. He stopped twenty yards from the burnt and debris-riddled barn. O'Hara measured the different distances in his head, how far from the main house to the barn, the barn to the second house, then the third. He didn't find what he wanted to. The houses were either too far or too close to the barn for all these men to be gunned down by a revolver. Too close, the men would've found the shooter and attacked or fled. Too far, and the shots should be sloppy. And they weren't.

When O'Hara inspected the second body nearest the barn, he figured the fire had been a decoy. "Like the bell," O'Hara muttered to himself. "All the men were rushing to the barn, but got shot at from another way." He ignored the other bodies for the moment and headed to the cabbage field. When he got there, the pigs squealed making O'Hara jolt back. He exhaled to calm himself, but it didn't do much for him. His heart was on a rampage, its thudding reaching into his ears. He suspected his wife's worries were getting to him. "Let's leave home at home," he said, trying to ground himself.

O'Hara scanned down the rows of cabbage until he saw the boot tracks. They were angled toward the barn and O'Hara was positive this had been the killer's position. "If you was here, being able to shot out in the open like ya did, it must have been dark too," O'Hara quickly realized. He knelt down to study a discolored cabbage near the boot track; it was blood, and the spots took him to Art's body which was laid out a couple feet from the wall of the main house. Another trail of blood spots went on farther, but O'Hara wanted to look at what was in front of him first. The body smelled of gun powder, so O'Hara

checked for any nearby firearms but, there weren't any. He noticed a few shotgun shells in the dirt beside the body, making
O'Hara believe that this fellow had had a gun, but figured the
killer must have taken it with him. O'Hara looked at the side
of the house and saw the blood that had dried over the paint.
Where the body was now, there wasn't any blood. Well, not
enough, O'Hara thought.

O'Hara guessed that with the blood not being at the body then
something wasn't straight. He rushed back to the other bodies and checked to see if the proximity of the bodies and blood
stains were reasonable. He confirmed his fear. All the bodies
had been moved. "I can't trust any of this," O'Hara concluded
dimly.

When O'Hara found the murdered Higgans in the kitchen
and Charles dead in his rocker he knew this was where the
killer had started. "He cleared out the main house first so he
could hold up in the cabbage field without worrying about anyone coming on his rear. You're deadly, cause you're smart." He
searched the house, finding two more bodies in a room with
scattered bottles and smokeware. The man had been shot in the
back in the head, and a fourteen-year-old girl had been shot
twice in the stomach. She was propped there on the wall when
O'Hara found her, her head sunk in her lap. He shifted the
bodies, looking for a gun, but didn't have any luck there either.
He did pick up a shell casing though, which had an "H" carved
into the brass and a gold hue to it. On the wall opposite the girl,
two rounds of shotgun pellets had been fired into the wood,
and there were blood stains in the carpet under it that didn't
seem to belong to those two. It just didn't make an inch of sense

for their blood to have gotten there when they had been shot up from the other side of the room. O'Hara knew this, and it caused him to weigh different scenarios. Could she have shot the killer here? But the blood out in the cabbage had to be the killer's. Either shot would have slowed him down to the point where he couldn't be doing all too much after. Was one of the Higgans an inside man? In the church the only victims were male, but here a young girl was killed. And she was the only victim with pellet wounds, instead of the revolver used on everyone else. It didn't sound like the killer. Were these two separate incidents, or had the killer been recruiting?

O'Hara wasn't sure what to think. His body twitched restlessly. His stomach coiled. He still had one trail to check up on, but his senses were pulling him away. He needed to follow the blood tracks near Art's body.

When he found them again he traced them out of the ranch and through the bear grass. O'Hara lost the trail a couple times, but was always able to find it again after doubling back. Finally, he came to the front of Vasquez Rocks. The unusual terrain put an immense pressure on O'Hara. The disadvantages of following someone into the rocks rolled off endlessly through O'Hara's head. Tight corners, multiple ridges all at different heights and angles, and the noisy gravel at the foot of the rocks all cried out danger to the Marshal.

The Marshal was on edge, never looking at the same spot for more than a few seconds. He crept on for about fifty yards, then froze at the sight of torn black cloth caught on the cliff's ridge. It waved with the breeze like a flag marking enemy territory. Then O'Hara heard the hammer of a pocket gun being set back. His hip had never felt so damn empty. "You are fixing to be killed." he thought. O'Hara scoured the area beneath him with a childish hope of finding something to save himself with. He believed he stood there for ten minutes, but that couldn't have been right. O'Hara finally held his hands up to his chest and fled back down the path.

Once he reached the perimeter of the rocks he sat so he could get control of his breath. Above, a cloud towered over him. It had an immense weight, as if it was a physical body that was positioned to collapse on him. His chest sunk.

———————

I TOLD THE POSTMAN to forward this letter on till it found you. I hope it does. I haven't got to speak with Maryanne yet. She is still shaken and it'll be best to wait on that. I did question most the of church survivors, though, and they all said much of what you already figured. Got a few things worth your time, Marshal, so that's why I sent this on.

Some said the killer asked about Delamar. It is a town not too far from this church, but my understanding is that it's been deserted since all that holler about mining died. A couple think he said something else, but what they said didn't make much sense when I thought about it. I already confirmed that some of the dead had lived in Delamar for a time. Make what you want of that. I know the Delamar Company still has a small steel operation in California north of Aqua Dulce. I'd check on that next.

Another thing about the man who did this: they all said he looked like a damn demon, missing his ears and most his teeth, and had scars up and down his face. I know when people go through something like this their minds make more of it than it actually was. People turn a man with a gun into the devil with hellfire if their fear gets a hold of em. A couple swore he jingled when he walked, a ring of metal or such. And others said he didn't walk, just hovered.

We already know he is a damn good shot, but from what the witnesses are going on about he might be better than what the scene led on. Not one man gave me the correct amount of shots fired. Most of them thought he fired thirty plus rounds, and more than half said that the gunshots went off so fast they can't remember how many there were. Like I said before, this could be the inflation of fear, and it probably is. But it makes me worry about you, Marshal. If you are to be a match to him, you ought to get a gun, and learn to shoot like that.

Earl and I followed the blood trail out. They stopped at tire marks. Earl thinks someone stole the body, and reason and logic will agree with him. It was miles out from the church. I got a thought, though. If I got shot and walked miles with a bullet in me I wouldn't be too keen on dying. Not then, anyway.

All this disturbs me. When I first started, we worried about people moving livestock, not some damn maniac. We had robbers and shootouts between cowboys and Indians and the law, but those all had lines. As low as it was, they had reason. I don't see reason in this. Reminds me of the war we in now and how the papers say this war we're in is the war to end all wars. That can't be true if men like this are out there. Men like this could start their own war.

-Sheriff Reed

———————

CHARLES HIGGANS VEERED his head back at the sight of the prisoner. Daniel used to be an alright-looking kid to Charles' mind, something that none of his own kids really had. A moveable cell had been positioned at the center of the mining town, and was nicer than his ranch house. Charles was particularly jealous of the full washroom and kitchen Daniel had open access to. A woman wearing a white blouse and long tan skirt glided to Charles inconspicuously. Her clothes were colored brilliantly and not faded by excessive wind or sand.

"Imagine keeping yourself like that," she breathed in his ear. Thinking he was alone with his thoughts Charles flinched at the noise.

"Daniel did this to himself?" he asked without confidence. The woman nodded as she removed a pocket fan and cooled herself. "Daniel," Charles called into the cage. Daniel sat at the farthest corner with his head in his lap. When their eyes met, Charles decided against asking him anything.

"He can't talk, you know, burnt his lips on water that he boiled. No accident, neither," she chimed in.

"That right, Miss Margot?"

Margot grimaced. "He did the whole nasty to himself. Banged his teeth out on the sink, scarred his face on the corner there." She stopped to wince at the thought. "My husband fit him with a fine cell, and that was after what he done—correct me, did, of course," she concluded.

"That's what the vote's about," Charles reminded.

"When he told me, I said no. Young Daniel would not do that to his own mother." She paused before continuing. "After keeping him, and seeing the things he did," Margot let her head fall on his shoulder, "I hate to say it, but it had to be him. His brain must have burned through," she sobbed.

The rest of the Higgans came and hollered what they thought of Daniel. Art studied him silently while the rest of the Higgans brothers mocked the prisoner. When his brothers had become bored, Art managed to sneak close to Daniel, and asked in a whisper, "Did you hurt yourself?"

Daniel shook his head in his lap, paying Art as little mind as he could.

"So you're saying Miss Margot is a liar. I know which way I am to vote. Your poor mother. I woulda had some pity for you if you had come clean to me," Art said with a venom lace. Daniel brought his face up and stared at Art as if to memorize it.

Art returned to his family when he couldn't stand Daniel's gaze anymore. Daniel looked at all the faces beyond his temporary cell, which was a facade designed to make him the monster. Before, Daniel wanted to fade away, to sit in the corner of the phony cell and hope death would take him. But when Art came and spoke, Daniel's heart stirred with malice. All of these faces were important. All these gentlemen appointed to vote for his life had no right.

When the whole town arrived and the voting was ready to commence, Daniel staggered to the front-facing bars and studied all of their faces. They were frightened, and Daniel was proud of it. And when each gentleman placed his vote in the ballot at the cell's foot he saw that face and remembered it.

672

DANIEL HAD NEVER SEEN a steel mill before, but he knew he was close when the sky disappeared and smoke took its place. He gazed up at the billowing clumps of darkened, artificial cloud, wondering if every steel plant ransacked the sky like this. His breath thinned gradually as he moved closer. The hike to the north side of the plant was more strenuous on Daniel's knee than he had thought it would be, and he had to rest it for about each half mile, all the while stressing the time he was losing.

On the north side, there was a back entrance with an overgrown trail leading to it, so Daniel figured it was seldom used. Above the entrance a sign fashioned from steel read "Delamar Steel." Daniel tried the door and was pleased that it was unlocked. He peered inside the plant and studied the overwhelming machinery and enormous vessels of iron. Black smoke that had fiery tinges from the molten light and other turbidities made it impossible to see to across the plant. Constant thudding and hammering followed by sharp sparking sounds numbed the eardrums. Open vats and burning slabs were scattered about unfenced. Daniel wondered if strolling through the plant picking off each steel worker as he went would be risk-free enough. If it wasn't for his knee, he thought he would have.

Mark was called over to stoves six and seven because the hot blast men were having a tough time changing the stove. These furnaces were the only two in the plant that were run completely on manual labor, so it wasn't all that uncommon that they would give the blast men trouble. Still, Mark dreaded working on those stoves. Everything was the thickest near them, from the airborne raw material to the heat that seeped past the protective head gear, it was unbearable. One of the blast men was always smoking his cigar as he went on, and the smoke would collect under his helmet like his personal black cloud. Mark never could figure how he was able to see, but the man would continue on with his work like nothing was different from him than the others. It wasn't like Mark could ask him or tease him about it, on account of that Mark only saw him down near stove seven and the iron process was far too loud to have a chat. Thing is, Mark realized he would never be able to joke with him about it when he arrived at stone seven and saw him lain across the ground—dead.

Mark thought it had been gas, or something of that nature, but then he saw the blood. Water was flowing down from the north ramp and around the body, curving on into the plant further. As the blood seeped within the water, it spread like paint because of the way it colored the water. Mark turned frantically to check his back, but no one was there. He breathed heavily, which he knew wasn't good for him, but he couldn't help it. Water was leaking in the steelworks, and he knew what that meant. He turned away from the running water and sprinted toward the plant's south-side exit, but stopped mid-way up on a steel stairway. If water was flowing down this way, it means it was coming from the north-side spigot. Mark couldn't decide if he should go there and cut the water off, or just run out with his life. Then he looked at his cigar friend's dead body. He had been shot dead. Mark continued up the steel ramp toward the south-side exit as quickly as he could, trying to mind his steps around any open vats and the such. His gear chafed and bounced about unevenly, nearly causing him to fall. When he got to the south-side exit he pushed through the doors, then immediately stopped at the pile of dead bodies at his feet. On the other side of those bodies was Daniel, who had his revolver ready to fire.

"I wondered if you were coming, Mark."

"The Hell is going on here?" Mark asked.

Daniel gestured with the nose of the revolver, and Mark raised his hands up past his shoulders.

"You know who I am?"

"We don't have no business. There ain't a reason for you to be doing this other than that you lost every decent part of your mind."

"Look," Daniel pointed at the mound of bodies at his feet.

Mark stared at the pile of men. Their blood had collected together under them, creating a crimson puddle. It was hard to distinguish the men on account of them being in their steel plant gear and them lying face-down toward Daniel in the dirt.

"Anything stick out to you?" Daniel asked.

"Yeah, they're dead, you son of a bitch!"

"Last words?"

Mark looked Daniel in the eye for a good while. He knew that there wasn't anything he could say or do to save himself, but Mark did think that if he was able to stall—perhaps just for five minutes if he was lucky—that the water might set off an explosion with power enough to kill the man in front of him. Rather take him with me, Mark thought.

"No? Alright." Daniel prepared to pull the trigger.

"Wait! I—I just don't know why you are doing this," Mark stammered.

"You know. All you Delamar gentlemen know. I thought for a second that I'd have to find you again. That you wouldn't come out this way. You did. Just like them all here, that's what they done. All you ever been is livestock." Daniel shot Mark clean through the heart, and he fell into the pile over the others.

Daniel put the pocket gun away and turned his back to the mess as he made his way from the plant.

O'HARA STOOD TWO-HUNDRED-or-so yards back from the plant and waited, keeping his eyes fixed on the building. The air was so clear he thought that he could see on forever. When he lost the feeling in his leg, he paced back and forth to get the blood to it again. A man with a white hat that was a size too large approached O'Hara from his rear, and O'Hara waved, but didn't turn around to greet him.

"You're the Marshal?" the man asked.

"Right," O'Hara replied, keeping his eyes on the plant.

The man gazed at the sky. "Never has it been like this." He then took off his hat and covered his eyes from the sun to look over to the north. "I imagine that is Washington up that'ta way."

"That hat you got does a better job at keeping the sun out."

"It was just for a bit of effect," the man replied, fixing his hair back before putting the hat on. He cleared his throat then continued, "All this difference in a day. Imagine if we didn't need the steel."

"There was a fair share of them back east, blackened the sky, made people sick, but it was a way of surviving. Some people ain't have options."

"I'm still right here, you know."

O'Hara nodded at him. "Don't come on following me now," the Marshal stated as he walked toward the plant.

"Sir—Marshal—it ain't safe yet. Not with the water leaking that was reported."

"Now what did I say."

"No disrespect, I ain't trying to ruffle you any wrong way. But you know what happens when water and molten steel mix right?"

"They don't mix, they blow up. The water is heated quickly and expands at an insane rate. It's called a steam explosion. Look, I am dealing with something that doesn't allow me to be wasting time. Have a good afternoon." O'Hara shook the man's hand hurriedly and turned back to the plant.

"I ain't your keeper."

O'Hara approached the south side of the mill and studied the pile of bodies outside the entrance. He flattened the pile by pulling each body out slowly. He flipped one body over to find where he had been shot—font chest. Another he flipped over, front chest. He did a third body, then decided that was how they all must had been done. O'Hara counted sixty-seven bodies once the pile was separated out. He walked about ten yards out from the pile and positioned himself to face the entrance, it had to be that easy for the killer. With how they were each shot in the front chest, they had to have just walked through the doors and been shot, O'Hara figured. "There was a bell, then a fire, so what will it be here?"

The Marshal eased the south entrance doors open. He didn't want to stir any of the reported water he had heard about. Just on the other side, tucked around the bend of the door, was a puddle of discolored water that had collected there without a way to drain. He studied the plant as a whole. It was small compared to the ones back east, but still complex enough. Some of the raw materials had a "Delamar Mine" label, one of which O'Hara ripped off and tucked in his suit pocket. He found the stairway to the overhanging platform and took that up so he could look down on the plant. He could see a handful of other bodies about eleven, to be exact. Some of the stoves were still hot and other than the puddle, there wasn't any water.

When he came back down to study the bodies up close he noticed that they had not all been shot in the chest. That made sense, the killer would have different angles in here. He checked the pockets, but didn't find anything interesting, a cigar cutter in one. O'Hara wasn't sure how the killer had gone about. He knew all of the killer's locations, but wasn't sure of the timing of it all. Not to mention how he had been able to get the better part of the workforce to leave out the south exit. Or even where the water had come from. "Let's start there," O'Hara decided.

The puddle had a brownish hue that was so congealed the Marshal was not sure of exactly what was polluting it. There was a cigar floating, and O'Hara gagged at the smell he brought out when he fished it out with his hand. The cigar was curled and shriveled from water damage, but O'Hara could tell it had been partway smoked before it had ended up here. O'Hara took the cigar to the man with the cutter in his pocket and noticed the cigar and cutter were both J.C. Newman Cigar products. "You dropped something, friend."

The Marshal knew there wasn't any sensible reason the killer could have had to move this man's cigar. Believing water had carried it, he came back to the puddle, then found the nearest upward slope and followed that path. It took him by the cigar man, but that wasn't what O'Hara was looking for. He continued till he reached the north side of the plant where a small, out-of-the-way exit door was positioned at the top of a rampway. Outside, only a few paces out, was a water spigot. The earth beneath it was muddy. He couldn't help but smile. "You always have a trick," the Marshal said aloud.

The spigot had been set closed, which surprised the Marshal. He couldn't think of a reason why the killer would hike back up the plant to turn off the spigot, especially with the possibility of the whole thing blowing to Hell. After a moment of thought, O'Hara wondered if perhaps one of the steel workers took this north exit. They would have been able to cut the water and might had survived the whole mess. O'Hara searched north of the plant, but didn't find anything. It bothered the Marshal that he couldn't come up with an idea, especially now that he knew how everything else on the scene had come to be.

When it got dark, O'Hara made his way back to the nearest town, where he ran into the man with the white hat again. The Marshal stopped him and showed him the "Delamar Mine" label he had found in the plant.

"Sure, sure. The Delamar Mine is where they shipped the materials in from. Why the interest?" the man asked.

"Thinking I'm going to make a visit. Sorry if I was cross with you earlier."

"Not a problem, Marshal, good luck on your case." The man and O'Hara shared a polite nod.

O'Hara contemplated how the spigot could had been shut off while he rested with his feet up on the motel bed, but then decided it was best to let it go and move on. He had learned early on that if you spend all your effort on one thing, all the other problems are going to take advantage. That wasn't the way the Marshal was going to run this case.

I WAS sittin watching the wind blow and decided I wasn't doing nothing useful. You would think, being as senior as I am, that I would know what to do to help with the case. That I had the process learned. It might surprise you that these past years it's been going out the other way yonder. And I ain't sure what is the best way to steer it back on trail. I like to tell myself that it just ain't my year. Well, that's bull crap. My wife, Nancy, she keeps telling me it's my age, like somehow getting older has made me lose touch. That might be on the nose. Fact is, she is right most of the time. But I got to wonder, if instead, it's the age. Times always change. We all know that, and we all think we are ready for it, but it came and went and knocked me on my ass. That's alright. I'll be on my feet soon enough, and you can remember I told you that.

Anyway, I know I ramble, but Maryanne still seemed pretty pale so I decided to visit this Delamar town the witnesses went on about. It's just one of those mining towns that emptied out as soon as the ore did. I found what you would expect to find in a deserted town; nothing. One thing kept reappearing, though, and that was the name of a Captian Joseph Delamar. There wasn't a paragraph written that didn't mention the man. Seemed like the town must have worshipped the Captain. "Loyalty to Delamar" and businesses that had "Partnered with Joseph Delamar." He could have been as popular as King Andrew Jackson. Even some of the text I read through talked of city laws and permissions being given from Joseph Delamar himself.

It got me curios, so I walked around some more, and there sticking out like an oasis in the deserted town was a fancy, high-dollar mansion. An older lady named Margot greeted me at the door, and I had to ask her how she was getting on living in, what my mind was, nowhere. A boy would run supplies once every two weeks she said. I asked if she was married, and it seemed like she didn't know how to answer it. But she said yes and gave me a peculiar look, so I thanked her for her time and went on my way. After that I had set out to poke around a bit more, but couldn't get over the foul taste that woman left in my mouth. A couple times I even glanced over my shoulder thinking I'd see her there following me. That was the extent of my trip, and I know it's about as useless as can get, but it's what I got.

What you're saying about the steel mill and how the killer went about is concerning me. I'll shoot straight with you; he isn't as smart as you're making him to be. When you hear a loud noise, you cover your ears and maybe shut your eyes. When something is burning, you rush off to put it out. When water is coming down from above, and it means danger to you, you run away from it, not up into it. Swim with the current, they say. It is the common behavior of people, that simple. There are few men who would do different. It's that animal in us that forces us to protect ourselves first. I told a man that same thing after breakfast the other day, and it got him pretty bothered. I think in my younger days if I heard an old grump go on like that I would take it as cynical nonsense too. I don't see it that way anymore. It is our nature, and that don't upset me.

I'll be waiting to see what you find out about the mine. I asked a man wearing a suit I couldn't afford what he thought of the same company owning a steel mill and the mine it got its materi-

als from, and he said it sounded like "pure wealth." Called it "vertical integration." I'll let you take a guess at what that means.

-Sheriff Reed

594

LEE STRAPPED THE TOOL belt around his waist and walked down the hallway of the mining outpost to test the fit. He made a great business about this, pacing back and forth. He tightened the buckle up an eyelet then trudged to the other end of the hall. After loosening the buckle again he started back, but stopped midway, irritated by a sharp wedge scratching at his hip.

When he arrived at the mine and walked past the hitching rail where a horse was tied he saw that Howard was waiting on him. Howard was in his fifties and had been working for the Delamar Mining Company since the first cart of rock had been filled and moved back in Delamar.

"You just got that belt," Howard criticized, pointing at the uneven eyelet that Lee had cut into the leather.

"It wasn't fitting right, sir. I'm real sorry 'bout it. I know it is company property and all, but I thought I wasn't doing all too much harm seeing as I would be the one keeping it, sir."

Howard shook his head then made his way into the mine, leaving Lee outside staring slack jawed at Howard's back.

"Keep up!"

Lee shuffled behind Howard, keeping a bit too close. At the foot of the mine, Howard lifted a pickaxe from a toolbox that had been conveniently placed there and a carbide lamp from the crate and gave them to Lee.

"Don't go putting holes in it, or sanding the bottom to make it shorter. Hurry on and get down the shaft," Howard indicated the direction with his coal-blackened hand before going on. "Already got workers down there, your father included."

Lee lit the carbide lamp and set off. The lamp shook between his clammy fingers. The air was cold and thin, with earthy particles that Lee had to cough out between breaths. There was an out-of-place smell Lee didn't like. As he continued the shaft narrowed. He worried he would scrape his head on the hard, uneven roofing, so he bent his knees slightly to avoid the possibility. The ground became uneven too. He hiked until he had to stop, panting and sweating. He thought the smell was stronger here. He sniffed a couple times; it smelled like gas, but he rationalized that it must be some type of ore he had never been around before. He looked back up the way he had come and wiped the sweat from his forehead.

When he started again, his foot slid on loose gravel, and he tumbled down. He did a decent job at rolling when he hit the ground so he didn't hurt himself too bad, but within the racket his tool belt had unbuckled and slid off down a side ramp. He rose shakily, spitting dirt out of his mouth when he got to his feet. He found his pickaxe and placed it up against a wooden support beam that held the mine's walls in place. Lee brought his hands to his hips and grimaced when he didn't feel his tool belt. He crouched with the lamp, panning over the crude stone and gravel to find the belt. He then brought the light up to a smaller shaft that ventured off from the main path. A sign was fastened between two horizontal planks partly blocking the path and it read "stay out and stay alive." Lee squatted under the wooden planks to enter the deserted shaft and searched the area with his lamp. When Lee's foot slid on sandy gravel, he feared dropping his lamp and being stuck in a closed-off section of the mine. He fastened the rope handles of the lamp across his chest and around his back. When he finished, he looked up. The lamplight revealed a mangled man looking back.

Daniel pointed his revolver at the frozen seventeen-year-old. They stared at each other.

"You don't work here," Daniel said.

"I start today with my pa and—"

"Stop," Daniel cut off Lee's quivering.

Lee couldn't think of what he was to do. The revolver was trained at his chest, and by the way the man in front of him looked in the lamplight, he thought the man had hiked up from Hell. Lee shifted his foot slightly; it nudged against the iron wedge. Its point came to a sharp edge that hadn't been dulled by use in the mines yet. Lee figured that it must have fallen out of his tool belt, wherever that had ended up.

"Your dad and all the others in here got to settle with me." Lee inched back. "Don't move," Daniel ordered.

"I don't think he owes you any money, Mister. You must be thinking of another fellow. Perhaps we can all sit down and talk about this," Lee suggested.

"That ain't on the table." They stood in silence for a moment. "You can keep your life," Daniel broke in. Lee listened, petrified. "Now get out and don't say nothing."

"You expect me to leave my pa?" Lee asked.

"He has a debt."

"Money don't got a thing to do with this, this revenge? Well he ain't kill no one, either. You got the wrong man."

"He took my life." Daniel locked the hammer back.

"You're standing right here," Lee argued.

"I don't call what I do now, living."

Lee was silent.

After taking a step forward, Daniel continued "There are over two hundred men below us, and they are meant to die. You smell the gas; I placed the last canister right here. I figure we are both lucky that lamp of yours has a glass seal." Daniel turned his hip so Lee could see the leaking gas canister tucked between a beam and the rock. It hissed. "It takes half an hour to go back out of here, and half to get to the bottom. That's an hour from the bottom up, or an hour and a half for you to find your dad and get out."

"Why you telling me this? If you're set to kill me, do it!" Lee pressed.

"In forty minutes I will ignite the gas and blow the cave; your dad will be buried. I'm telling you that you can either be buried with him or fix him a nice gravestone and take care of your ma. You don't have a debt with me," Daniel concluded.

"Do all the people that you're gonna kill by blowing the mine, do all of them have a debt to you?" Lee already knew the answer.

"Most of them," Daniel said reluctantly.

"You son of a bitch! You're out to kill everyone, me included. But you can't pull that right now trigger, or you might kill yourself in the mine. Just like we are lucky about this lamp being sealed and not blowing that gas, that trigger, one spark, spells our death."

"It's as good a time as any," Daniel bluffed.

Lee contemplated his options, which he figured were not all that great. "Okay," Lee gave. He started back, digging the heels of his boots into the ramp which he had come down. The nose of the Iver Johnson followed Lee as he took each rigid step back.

Lee shifted the toe cap of his boot under some loose gravel and kicked it up. Daniel shielded his eyes from the sand and the rocky pebbles with his forearm. Lee slid down the ramp and got the wedge in his hand, then stuck it through the fatty part of Daniel's calf. Daniel's leg buckled and his still-tender knee skidded against the rigid stone beside Lee. Lee turned his back to scramble away from Daniel, but was held back when Daniel caught Lee's ankle with his free hand. Lee rolled to his back to stomp Daniel's teeth in, but as his head turned, it met the steel butt of Daniel's revolver.

When Lee came to, the gas had overcome most of the breathable air. His head pounded, and one of his eyes wouldn't open. Dried blood from the blunt wound on his forehead had crusted over his left eye. One of his pant legs had been cut to his knee as well, leaving it half the length of the other leg. He rubbed his leg and felt around the calf, no wound. The man was gone, and the mine hadn't blown yet.

Lee pulled his shirt up over his nose to try to ward off the stagnant air as he stumbled his way back up the ramp. He stood at the cross between where the mine went up and where he could continue down for his father. His legs wouldn't move.

Daniel limped up the trail coming to the entrance where he could see sunlight breaching into the mine. His leg was wrapped with the torn-off portion of Lee's pant leg, which was now completely soaked through with blood. Howard heard boots dragging across the rocky ground and called out from his post.

"Thirty minutes early for lunch," Howard protested.

"Get the doctor!" Daniel cried.

Howard bounced out of his chair and sprinted out from his post without looking back. Injuries were common place in the mines, and Howard had learned that acting quickly was critical. When he made it to the hitching rail he thrust himself on his horse and sawed through the rope with his pocket knife. The horse had galloped twenty yards out from the hitching rail when Daniel had made it out to the surface. The sun was blinding to Daniel, but he already had the revolver out and fired it as quick as he spotted Howard riding off. Howard's body slumped over the horse's side as it raced on. Daniel didn't like that much. He thought that shooting a man in the back was becoming a common practice of his, but he also thought about what Howard had said moments ago. Thirty minutes early for lunch meant that the employees of the Delamar Mining company were already on their way up. And, depending on the ground they had already covered, Daniel wasn't sure if he could get in position to set the mine off in time.

Lee ran down the mine shaft yelling out as the light strapped to his chest bounced wildly. Every second felt like it was going to be his last before an explosion would trap him in death. "Dad!" he screamed again.

"Lee?" it was his father's voice coming from around the bend. When Lee made it around the cave's turn, his father was leading a group of miners up. It was a miracle; Lee knew they should have been far deeper in the mine.

"You're late. It's already break. I stuck my neck out for you. Dammit, Lee!" his father accused. Lee rushed closer and when his father saw the crusted blood caked down his son's face, his irritation left.

"What is this?"

"We have to go—there's a gas leak! We are dead here!" Lee cried between his panting. The miners panicked. They were the first group taking lunch; a few miners said they needed to go get the others.

"It's done, too late for them. We gotta get with our lives," called a miner. Lee's father agreed.

"That ain't right!" Lee argued.

His father grabbed him around his waist and steered him forward.

"No, Christ, let me get em! They're gonna suffocate!" Lee begged. His father and the others pushed Lee on, who was too worn to put up a good fight.

Daniel hobbled up the side of the hill, which was topped with coarse, metamorphic, rock. From this height, he could see the curved path that led to the mine's entrance at the hill's base. He had to climb on all fours to get to over the cliff where the mountain evened out. In the middle of the flat peak was the ventilation shaft, a tire-wide hole that stretched down to the bottom of the mine that allowed for airflow. Daniel steadied himself against the inner cavity where hard, protruding clay provided a ridge. He gripped his revolver, then readied it out from his coat pocket and fired down the shaft.

When the bullet struck the side of a rock, sparks lit the gas and a fire engulfed the mine. The wooden beams collapsed as shards of stone splintered out from the eruption. The mountain caved in beneath Daniel, flinging him to the ground and pinning his arm in the ventilation shaft. Flames roared out of the shaft and bit Daniel's fingers, causing his hand to open and drop the revolver. After a last pull Daniel freed his hand and turned to his back looking at his forearm, which was bubbling and blackening from the flames.

Lee and his father had made it to the mine entrance about ten yards ahead of the group, but hadn't left the shade of the cave. Lee smiled with relief. His father turned back from the cave's entrance and smiled back. The explosion popped Lee's eardrums before throwing him the ground, and his father was knocked back at that instant as well. When he got to his feet, Lee's father saw his son pinned beneath the rocks that had collapsed with the explosion. The hill had crumbled into itself. Everyone in the tunnel had been crushed to death.

"Lee! Lee!" his father screamed as he ran close. Lee was alive. He looked up at his father, pale and frightened. Lee's jaw had been crushed between the rubble and earth. He couldn't speak. Instead he made painful grunts. His father shifted through the rubble, pulling rocks and gravel out from above Lee.

"Help! Someone help!" his father begged, "My boy's gonna die!"

A man approached the rubble with a strained walk.

"Look, help's coming, Lee! Hang on!"

Lee fussed, letting out a frenzy of unintelligible wails. His father did all he could, hastily deciding what rocks to pull at despite fearing that he could cause the rubble to shift in a way that might further injury Lee. When the man came behind Lee's father, he took the bloodied iron wedge from his coat pocket and pierced it through the miner's neck. Lee helplessly watched his father die.

"I gave you a chance," Daniel said with emotion tuning his voice a pitch higher. "If I had my gun, I'd shoot you so the pain would be done. Sorry."

Lee needed a way out. He begged for God, so he could lift the weight and give Lee another chance. Lee knew that the man was right. He had been given one chance. But it wasn't one the man had given him, it was the one he had had when they had been together in the mine. He had let it spoil when he didn't stab the man through the heart with that iron wedge. If he had another chance, he wouldn't waste it. He prayed for a second chance, but those don't come.

O'HARA ARRIVED ON THE scene and did his usual work through the night, but he needed sunlight before he could tell anything. Seemed like the whole town had shown up to see what was left of the mines, and they grieved in the dark when they understood what was in front of them. The sun had just begun rising, but its light didn't reveal anything, or give any hope. The mine was nonexistent—every entrance had been caved in from the explosion. Families of the miners dug and called for their husbands or boys, but nothing would come of it. A few of them were sent off to try for the doctor again. Fact was, he hadn't been at his home since the incident. No one had any idea where he might be, but everyone agreed it was a hell of a time to be unreachable. O'Hara wasn't at all concerned about a doctor being present, though. Everyone was dead. O'Hara knew that.

O'Hara found a single body outside the entrance; it was an older miner whose neck had been pierced through by an iron wedge. Most the people gathered at the incident thought the whole thing had been an accident, a gas leak or some sort that had caused the hill to collapse. But this miner was killed outside the mine, meaning the whole thing was preconceived mass murder. He was just a tad luckier than the rest—he had gotten to die quickly. There were some sorry souls that had been trapped in the mine's cavities and suffocated. O'Hara didn't think on it too long, it was making him uneasy.

As far as the scene went all the Marshal had was one body that didn't give him any idea of what to do next. This was O'Hara's dead end. He had been lucky enough before to get a lead from Maryanne and another from Reed, but his luck seemed to be out. Where had this man set off to now? Two hours and O'Hara couldn't come up with a damn guess. Was this it? Had his killer rigged the mine to blow with him inside and taken everyone with him? "No, the dead miner with the wedge through his neck meant the killer made it outside, and was walking," O'Hara concluded.

"The doctor still ain't at his house! And Howard is there shot dead on his roan!" a boy cried aloud when he returned.

O'Hara was pointed in the direction of the doctor and set out. He drove west till he spotted the lonesome adobe shack that rested at the foot of a clay hill. The roan had Howard slung over its side and was whining at the cabin's door which had been left ajar. O'Hara got Howard's foot loose from the stirrup and let his body fall to the dirt. "Shot in the back as you rode off, and the horse kept on till it got to the doctor," O'Hara thought as he patted the horse's neck.

The cabin was cluttered with medical papers and illustrated diagrams of human anatomy. They were scattered about the cabin's floor and the desk. It was odd—every other aspect of the living space was well kept and fashioned. Along the walls were neatly labeled filing cabinets, and the furniture was set in a particular way, as if the person who had arranged it had put a good deal of time into it. When the Marshal made his way to the dresser drawers and opened each one he only found an undershirt and three socks that were cramped up at the back of the drawer.

O'Hara took these as obvious indications that the doctor had left in a hurry. He scanned through all of the doctor's documents which took a good deal of time, but the labor paid him well. One sheet had the doctor's name and home address in Los Angeles; Dr. Andrew Ryan had been contracted out to the mine, and it wasn't his first time working for Delamar, neither. He could have a history with Delamar, which means he was either one of the bodies that was buried in the mine, or he was running with death at his britches. The way O'Hara saw it, the doctor was running. Even if O'Hara was wrong, Dr. Ryan and the killer were connected, meaning it was worth the Marshal's time to investigate. A second document was a blueprint of the mine. O'Hara figured the best way the mine could be set off while keeping yourself alive would be the ventilation shaft. He knew it wasn't too likely, but checking that shaft might lead him to something.

When he made his way back to the mountain, it was a quarter past noon. He climbed up the side and found loose dirt at the top, which he figured must be covering the shaft. After shoveling earth up with his hands, he came to the shaft's opening and cleared the dirt from its mouth completely. He peered in the shaft and saw something glint in the sun. It was ten yards deep in the shaft and had been caught up by a rock that had moved during the explosion. He borrowed a rope and hook from an onlooker and lowered it at a snail's pace into the shaft. He played with it for half an hour before he felt the hook catch onto the object. He brought it up and looked at the glinting metal dangling on the roped hook. It was a five-chamber Iver Johnson revolver.

From the top of the mountain looking down O'Hara noticed a trail in the dirt that stretched out west a few yards from the mine then stopped, as if a dead animal had been dragged out from the entrance. O'Hara was able to spot where the trail ended and he planned his path over the mountainside before descending. At the trail's end, there was a fresh mound of dirt that the Marshal thought could make for a rushed grave. O'Hara brushed dirt off the mound till he uncovered an eye encrusted with dried blood. O'Hara sat on the sandy-pebbled ground with the revolver in his hand and stared at the half-buried boy that looked about half the Marshal's age. Here again, like the girl O'Hara had found shot dead at the ranch, was a victim that didn't fit. He was too young to be from Delamar. O'Hara couldn't make sense of why this boy had been killed, dragged out, and buried. It was what a person does in remorse. O'Hara couldn't imagine the killer had that kind of opinion about his own handiwork.

After he cleared the dirt, the Marshal was looking at Lee, but he didn't know it. The legs had been crushed, and the lower jaw was broken off from his skull. A shotgun round had been fired into his heart as well. After digging around the body a bit more, O'Hara found the shell, which had an "H" engraved into the brass. "Just follow the breadcrumbs."

When the Marshal came back to town he picked up the daily paper and skimmed through it as he walked to his Model T. A headline made him stop. "Mad Killer Hunts Delamar Residents."

———————————————

I SHOULD BEGIN BY ASKING your pardon, Marshal. I reckon you read the paper, and I can't imagine you being all too happy by what's written in there. Fact, I bet you are damn upset about it. A reporter asked me the about the church, and I told her I wasn't giving any case details up. She was nice enough, just trying to make a name for herself, I imagine, but she offered to pay me for the information, and I told her to kindly go push sand. Yeah, to no point, though, Earl took her up on that pretty eagerly. He must have.

He knew I wouldn't have him anymore because of it. He tried to buy his job back with the money he got. Said that "a witness would'a gave the story for nothing and that this money could help." That, or he is a damn crook who ain't better than swine. He gave me all the money he said he got, which was more than I expected that lady had been capable of paying, but I don't put him above hiding half of it under his mattress. Anyway, I'm real embarrassed this came from my yard. And before you say it wasn't my fault, I say if you are a bad enough boar none of the little piggies would think about squealing.

Now it is about where you move from here. This will reach Delamar residents, which may be a good thing, but it will also reach the killer. I don't need to say how bad that is. Best of luck, Marshal.

I plan on visiting your wife like you asked after I send this out. I'll write you next about how that goes. And I meet with Maryanne tomorrow; I'll detail that in my next writing as well, Marshal. As one lawman to another lawman, let me say this without disrespect, Marshal. What happened in Higgans' ranch and the mill, you couldn't had changed it if you wanted to. You have to accept that.

-Sherriff Reed

SHERRIFF REED'S BOOTS announced his approach up the porch steps and toward the front door. Stella softly rose from the rocker when she heard the hollow knocks of his boot heels from inside the house. She positioned herself behind the front door, with her knees slightly bent and a cast-iron frying pan cocked behind her shoulder. Reed was straightening his bolo tie and tucking his shirt in properly when Stella called out from behind the door, "I was not expecting any company, so I will not be having it! There is a barrel of our coach gun aimed at your groin! And yes, I said "our," so if you have any education, you will conclude that me and my husband, a US Marshal, mind you, are more than willing to shoot off your boys!"

"Now, Mrs. O'Hara, I don't mean you any annoyance," Reed assured.

Stella let out a low grunt, cleared her throat in a rugged guttural fashion, then spoke with a decent impression of the Marshal. "Stella, gal, shoot them boys off of that deaf gentleman will ya now?"

Responding to the impersonation of her husband with her soft, natural voice, Stella shouted, "You said it, Hon!"

"Ma'am, O'Hara asked me to ride by and—"

"I never asked a thing like that," Stella voiced as the Marshal.

"I knew it, you lying piece of stewing crap!" Stella cursed in her own voice.

"Ma'am, I'm Sheriff Reed. The Marshal wrote to me about you," Reed responded.

"That right?"

"It is, ma'am"

"He wrote you, and he hasn't wrote me once."

"I can't speak for him, but he has written me."

"Are you sweet on him?"

"The Marshal?"

"He must be sweet on you if he is writing you and not his wife."

"No, ma'am."

"No to you being sweet on him, or him being sweet on you?"

"Well, Mrs. O'Hara, my last answer is fine for both those questions."

"That right?"

"Yes, ma'am."

Stella placed the pan on the stand beside the door, then asked, "Do you think he is foolish?"

"He is an intelligent man. With all respect, I imagined you to know that first hand," Reed said with an honest grin.

"I said 'foolish.' Do you think he is being foolish?"

"It's a fine thing he is doing."

Reed stood outside the door for a few seconds. He gathered Mrs. O'Hara was a witty gal and figured she deserved a frank response. "It is a bit foolish, ma'am."

"At least a bit foolish!" Stella then eased the door open, finally revealing herself to the Sheriff.

Reed looked her up and down, then responded with a charm that a handful of older gentlemen seem to acquire with age, "I think he is a damn fool." After he said that, she had a nice smile that didn't want to go.

Stella prepared tea for the Sheriff and herself and they sat out on the porch for the remainder of the visit. She would ask a few things about the case, which got her worrying about the Marshal, and then she wouldn't want to hear more of it. To get her mind at ease, she would ask about Reed and his home life for a spell, until she guided the questions back to the case. "It won't ring out, I told him it won't, Sheriff." After repeating this to Reed and, frankly, repeating it to herself, Stella would abruptly ask something along the lines of, "Do you think the weather will shape up?" This would start up her cycle of conversation again, and Reed caught onto the format of it all rather quick.

He wasn't sure if Mrs. O'Hara had been enjoying his visit or was aggravated from it. But she was talkative, so at least he was someone to be talked at. After Stella had gone through her wooden routine for a fourth time or fifth time—Reed had stopped keeping count—the Sheriff asked her, "Do you know why Marshal O'Hara won't carry?"

Stella stopped for a moment, searching for her words. "I do."

"Wasn't my intention to be nosey, Ma'am."

"It's alright, Sheriff."

"I apologize."

"No, you weren't prying so save your apology." Stella took a peek at the Sheriff's mug; it was half full.

"Tea? You're half out," she said as she stood.

Reed thought he had had plenty of tea already, and plenty left in his tin mug, but accepted the offer kindly. As Stella filled his tin she added, "He has good reason." The Sheriff nodded.

When Reed made his leave, he realized that he had spent too much of the day with Mrs. O'Hara and wouldn't be able to make the drive out to Maryanne till Sunday morning. "It'll just have to be patient," he thought as he walked from the porch.

"I'll have tea in the kettle for this Saturday," Stella called from the doorway. The Sheriff turned back and smiled at the lady, amused by what he hadn't been expecting to hear.

ANDREW RYAN SAT ALONE on the corner of Broadway and Slauson as he thumbed through the daily paper. He had placed an empty mug on the edge of the table for the waitress to see, and when she dropped off a fresh mug, Andrew avoided eye contact. The table was cramped, so he had to lift his mug and place the folded newspaper under it with the front page facing out. The cover of the L.A. Times read "Delamar Beware! Church Shot Dead!" He crossed his legs under the table and his knee bumped the table's underside when he did, bumping the coffee mug off to the sidewalk where it shattered. Andrew knelt and used his kerchief to wipe the coffee from his wingtip shoes. After he cleaned up the best he could, a man sat across the table.

"Don't look so stupid. You knew I was coming," said the man.

"Startled me. That's all," replied Ryan.

"Christ sake," the man snapped.

"He is still out there, you said he—"

"I know what I said."

"You lied."

"I was told he died. Then I shared the information with you."

"Now you were told, before you said you saw him dead with your own eyes."

"Doctor, I know what I said." The man leaned over the table, letting his pointed eyes set on the doctor. "Take a breath."

The waitress put her hand on the table to let the gentlemen know she was back. "Will you be having a coffee too?" she asked the man.

The man rested his hand over hers and smiled, placing his eyes on her for a moment. "Unfortunately I can't stay long darling. But go on and take that and don't bother about bringing it back," he slid the twenty-dollar bill into her palm and cupped her fingers around it.

"Oh, why, thank you very kindly, sir," she said, clearly flustered, trying to order her words that all wanted to come out at once.

"My pleasure." He caressed the back of her palm with his thumb before letting go. She insisted that he should come back and ask for her by name, and then went on about tending to the other tables.

Dr. Andrew Ryan watched on with a pale face; his leg shook. The man gripped the fleshy part above the doctor's knee and pressed his thumb and forefinger deep into the sensitive veins.

"Stop shaking," he ordered.

The pain made it click for Ryan. He took a breath, and the blood returned to his face.

"Let's be the smart, capable men that everyone in Delamar knew us for."

Ryan nodded.

"Have you kept the records?" the man asked.

"Yes, all of the medical records on everyone who lived in Delamar are in my office. I know you told me most of the polices had lapsed, but you also told me to keep them so I have," assured the doctor.

"Excellent. Update them."

"Okay."

"I died of old age, two years ago. Put that in my file."

"And the misses?"

"She died last year, Model T accident"

"Okay."

"First thing you do."

"I understand."

"My file first. Understand?"

"Yes, what about—"

"You see the briefcase?"

Dr. Ryan darted his eyes to a briefcase beside the man's foot.

"It is topped with American dollars," continued the man. "Something I learned over the years, money buys anything, anyone, and it'll buy revenge too."

"I'll handle it."

"Yes, you will." The man pushed in his chair and left.

366

THE SUN WAS STILL LURKING under the horizon when the Sheriff came to Maryanne's door. Reed knew she would be dressed and ready for the morning service despite what had happened, and he wanted to talk to her before she got on her way. Maryanne let Reed in and asked him to sit, then sat across from him, only to start up as soon as she did.

"Oh, where are my manners. Coffee?" Maryanne asked, and then went to the kitchen before waiting for an answer.

"That is quite alright, ma'am. My wife had some for me when I woke."

"Right, sure, sure." Maryanne returned to the couch, stood up again to smooth her dress, and then sat back. She fidgeted her fingers together, rubbing at her skin as if to clean it.

"Now, ma'am, I'm only here to ask a few questions."

"Excuse me, Sheriff, if you don't mind. The coffee was more for myself," Maryanne broke in.

"No you don't." Reed stood from his seat before she could, and he motioned her to stay; he made his way to the kitchen and heated the coffee. When the Sheriff had the hot tin in his hand he came back to Maryanne who was now quivering. He held her hand and guided it to take the tin, then sat facing her. She went to sip the coffee, but her hand shook and a dab spilt on her dress. The tin would have completely poured out if Reed hadn't caught it from her hand and set it down.

"Sheriff, I'm scared."

"Only natural after what happened."

"It's more than that, Sheriff." Maryanne sniffled.

"It's a lot more than anyone was expecting, especially myself."

"No! You're not listening, Sheriff!" Maryanne fell to her knees and sobbed into her cupped hands. Reed shifted forward in his seat.

"Back in Delamar, we all knew what was going on to that boy. We created him, and my hands aren't clean! None of us did a thing, and all the men voted him to his death, to protect the Captain. I know it now and it's too late and God won't help us."

Reed slid off of the chair onto the floor and knelt close to Maryanne.

"His name is Daniel. He was wronged, and God knows it. I think God might, yes, he wants this. He wants us to pay our due, and Daniel is his usher."

"A U.S. Marshal is doing what he can."

"But that ain't it, Sheriff! When I left the church, I nearly ran over a dead body, or I thought he was dead, till I got out and he was breathing and bleeding." Maryanne winced before continuing. "It was Jesse: he was hysterical and going on about his pa saying he had no reason to die."

"Where is he?"

"That's the issue, Sheriff; I kept him here for a day till he felt better then..."

"Where did he head?"

"It's my fault, Sheriff,"

"Where is he?"

"He wouldn't be if I didn't."

"Maryanne!"

Maryanne stopped crying and her face faded from a flush red to cold white. She wiped her tears then said, "I told him about Higgans' ranch, and Jesse went off after him."

"When?"

"A day after it..."

Reed stood up and went to the washroom and scrubbed his face with water and a rag. He leaned his back against the wall, took a cigarette, and lit it. He watched it burn for a moment before setting it between his chapped lips. Jesse had left for the ranch a day before the Marshal had; the Marshal's letter began making a lot of sense. This boy from Delamar whom God sent was killing men from Delamar, not a fourteen-year-old girl on a ranch. He wasn't moving bodies, neither. Jesse was coming between Daniel and the Marshal and if it goes as foul as the Sheriff was imagining, then the Marshal might shoot Jesse dead in Daniel's place.

EARL LOOKED OUT THE window at the Sheriff who was marching up the bar porch. Earl grabbed his coat and asked the barkeep, "You got a back door?"

The barkeep pointed at a far corner, but the Sheriff entered and called for Earl before he could slip out.

"Sheriff, I'm real sorry," Earl explained.

"Sit the hell down," Reed pulled a chair out from a table, letting its legs drag against the floor. Earl glanced at the chair, then sat.

"I can leave town if that'll be better," Earl suggested with a slight quiver.

"I'm leaving town," the Sheriff barked. Reed then slammed Earl's old piece and badge on the table. "If I had anyone else who could, I'd put them to do this. But I don't. I need to speak to the Marshal in Los Angeles, and I'll be back when I can."

"I can't do this on my own, Reed."

"I don't care if you can or can't. You're doing it. And when I make my way on back you better pray I'm feeling agreeable." Reed set his eyes on Earl till the Sheriff figured Earl wasn't going to say anything then made his way to the door. When Reed was out of sight from the front window, Earl ordered a glass of house whiskey.

When the door swung open again Earl nearly spit out his whiskey thinking the Sheriff had come back. But there, standing in the doorway with the light at her back, was a pretty woman with curls that inched past her shoulders. "You seen Sheriff Reed? I heard he is on his way to see my husband."

———————

THE MARSHAL ARRIVED early Sunday before the morning warmth had set in. The doctor had an address downtown on the fifth story of a building that served the finer people in life. O'Hara climbed up the marble staircase, annoyed by the clacking sound his boots made as he stepped. He knocked on the doctor's room, and then after knocking again he let himself in. After glancing around the Marshal was sure that the doctor was in Los Angeles. No dust, the bed was partly made, and it smelled like someone too. O'Hara helped himself to a mug of coffee, then combed through documents that were left on a desk. The documents were patient files, detailing date of birth, medical history, and current address. All the records originated in Delamar, and some of the patients had already been marked with a date of death. A good portion of the files recorded a time of death; they totaled **287**. For the files that recorded a death, they also stated whether or not a benefit was paid, which the Marshal knew was common practice for group insurance plans. All the papers were ordered chronologically from 'living' to 'dead,' except for the top two files.

A Captain Joseph Delamar and his wife Margot Delamar sat at the top of the records. According to the medical files Joseph had died of natural causes two years ago and his wife a year after due to a car accident. The Marshal wasn't buying. He pulled another file from the stack, a person who had died two years back due to a cough. O'Hara compared the ink of both files and found that the markings on the Captain's file were all too fresh and shiny, same as his beloved's file. O'Hara thought that these two files must had been written up not even a week before, and they had been placed on top hollering to be seen.

When the Marshal was done with the search he poured the rest of the coffee, which had become cold from neglect, and cleaned up any trace he may have left before exiting. He sat at a table across the street from the apartment and ordered an early lunch which a soft-faced waitress brought out. She smiled at the Marshal, and so he made a business out of showing his ring when he inched the plate of food closer to his chest.

He stayed outside the apartment till nightfall, moving from one street corner to the next to keep attentive and out of general suspicion. A man standing across from the apartment caught his interest. He had on quite a trench coat for how warm the night was, and he just stared at the apartment with his right hand clutching a bulge in his coat. O'Hara had the opinion that it was the barrel of a shotgun, but needed to confirm one way or the other.

After two hours when the streets emptied, O'Hara sat at a bench next to the man and waited. He eventually bent his head to face the man and asked for a cigarette. The man apologized for not having one and dismissed the Marshal.

"You're up quite late, aren't ya?" the Marshal said.

"If you say so," the man replied, staring ahead.

"Help me out here. If you don't have a smoke, maybe you have something else," O'Hara prodded.

The man ignored O'Hara. O'Hara peered at him for a moment.

"Seems like you're caught up. I apologize for being a pest."

"Don't go apologizing," The man looked at O'Hara for the first time. "Here," the man opened his coat to fetch the flask that stuck out slightly from the inner breast pocket and as he did, O'Hara got a glimpse of the shotgun.

After sipping from the flask of warm gin O'Hara handed it back to the man and thanked him. "That's a fine piece you got. Fact I got mine the other day," The Marshal flashed the Iver Johnson revolver.

"That right?"

"And I bring it up cause they were selling shells for that shotgun of yours two blocks down for half of what they worth. Owner cursed that he couldn't get em off his shelves. And he can engrave them too. Never heard of engraving a shell."

"Never heard of it?"

"No, and I don't believe it, either."

"You should."

"Not like you have seen one."

"Sure have."

"You're fooling," O'Hara turned out into the street, pretending to be done with the conversation. Not a quarter of a minute went by before the man flaunted a shell pinched between his thumb and forefinger. The man rotated it slowly to reveal an engraved "H" on the brass.

"Now I'm the fool. Mind if I ask your name?"

"Jesse. And don't be hard on yourself; fact is, I only found these the other day on this trashy ranch."

The Marshal put the nose of the revolver against the side of Jesse's knee. "Drop the smoke-pole."

Jesse's leg tensed up. He was barely able to see the revolver against his knee. "What's this about?"

"It's about keeping a leg or not." O'Hara positioned himself behind Jesse and slid his foot between the other man's to trap him there.

"Alright, ease up," Jesse noticed the Marshal's foot between his. "I'll drop it." Jesse positioned the shotgun where he wanted it then let go.

The bulk of the gun fell on O'Hara's foot, and he flinched at the sudden pain of it. Jesse twisted his body to the Marshal, striking him across the cheek with his fist, then grabbed his shotgun and ran off. O'Hara stumbled up from the bench chasing after Jesse.

"U.S. Marshal! Stop!" O'Hara ordered. After the first block O'Hara was gaining on Jesse, and it wouldn't be long till he caught up. Jesse turned the loaded shotgun and fired at the Marshal. O'Hara dove into the street, scratching his elbow on the uneven brick and rolled as he landed, avoiding a second shot that sparked beside him. O'Hara ended his roll with his elbows propped on the brick and the revolver's sights at his eye set to fire. He had a perfect shot pinned on Jesse, until the light of an approaching Model T blinded the Marshal and forced him to roll back to the sidewalk. Jesse turned into an alley and out of the Marshal's sight. O'Hara followed.

Jesse panted and shook while he opened the shotgun to load shells as he ran through the alley. One of the shells bounced out of Jesse's hand and into the darkness where it was lost immediately as the Marshal rounded the alley. Jesse closed the shotgun and swung back to face the Marshal who, hearing the snap of the gun, ducked around the alley corner. The first shot fired, and the Marshal waited for the next, but it didn't come. He lay on the ground and poked his head into the alley at knee-level to avoid eating shotgun pellets. He caught a glimpse of Jesse turning the alley to head back in the direction they came, but on the parallel street. The Marshal headed back down on his street toward the doctor's apartment, checking across each alley for Jesse and spotting him after the third alley.

DANIEL PAID THE MAN behind the counter, who slid the keys to him and some coin change. When Daniel got to his room he fetched the chair that was sitting beside the bed and placed it at the window. The wall clock read 11:10 before noon. Daniel sat on the chair and stared out the corner window at the downtown intersection beneath him. He scanned the streets and checked the entrance of the building where the doctor's address was. Daniel then took a revolver from a hidden holster beneath his coat and cleaned it.

The Marshal stepped out of the doctor's building five minutes later, and Daniel recognized him to be the man who had followed his trail into the Vasquez Rocks. Daniel figured he was a lawman and watched him cross the street and order lunch. Daniel sat all day, watching him wait at different corners of the crosswalk, wondering at what point would the lawman call it a wash. Daniel considered shooting him, and realized that Vasquez Rocks would had been the best time for that, but Daniel decided he wasn't going to kill a good man less he had to. "Don't make me have to."

As night fell, Daniel saw Jesse staring at the doctor's building. Daniel was confident that he had shot Jesse in the leg and figured he would had been buzzard feed by now. Daniel grimaced, then looked at the lawman who was spying on Jesse.

When the Marshal sat beside Jesse, Daniel knew the lawman had the wrong idea. Daniel put his gun in his holster and left his room to wait downstairs where he watched the two until they started shooting, and as they ran off, Daniel walked across the street and into the doctor's building.

Daniel forced the lock and eased the door closed behind him. His gun was drawn and his finger was curled around the trigger as he paced through the rooms. At a desk, he found the doctor's files stacked just as the Marshal had. Daniel brought them up to his face and read the Captain's file. Daniel slammed the butt of his revolver against the corner of the desk splintering the wooden corner apart.

"It isn't fair, Daniel," sounded a sympathetic voice from the kitchen.

Daniel whipped around, guiding the barrel's sights to the doctor's neck while his burnt right hand still clutched the files.

"He did terrible things, and we let him," Dr. Ryan admitted. "I should have done more."

"I'll kill you for damning me," cursed Daniel.

"The Captain is dead, this is pointless."

"That bastard died of natural causes!" Daniel fired three rounds into the ceiling above the doctor. Sawdust floated down.

"I have thought a lot about who I was then, and how weak we were to the Captain. But that doesn't give me a pardon. I don't know how to phrase this, but, take this and leave this mess behind." The doctor brought the briefcase up to his chest.

"The Captain is dead. My escape, and the innocents I killed, are for nothing if I can't throw the Captain atop the grave of Delamar!"

"By the innocents you mean some of the miners, don't you, Daniel," the doctor concluded. Daniel stared with boiling tears welling in his eyes. "I'll tell you what you can do. Deposit this money to an organization and name it after your mother. Send a share to the innocent families. Buy a boat and never come back to this country." Then Dr. Ryan set the briefcase on the kitchen counter and paced to the door.

"Don't." Daniel had the revolver back on the Doctor and was intent on firing.

"There wouldn't be any meaning in that, Daniel." Dr. Ryan closed the door softly behind him and left Daniel where he stood.

Jesse sprinted past the street lamps as he made his way back to the doctor's building. A fog began to fill downtown which made the light from the streetlamps seem to materialize within the density. When he turned onto the street that would intersect with the corner of the doctor's building, he looked behind him and was relieved that the fog sheltered him from the pursuing Marshal. As Jesse approached he could make out a faint figure in the fog.

The Marshal grimaced as the fog thickened to the point where spotting Jesse through the alleys wasn't viable. O'Hara had to trust that Jesse was rounding his way back to the doctor's apartment, though the Marshal hated putting his chips on a hunch when his man was so close. But as he approached the intersection he could make out two figures in the fog. The Marshal knew the one coming from the intersecting street had to be Jesse, and O'Hara readied his gun.

Daniel stood in the middle of the intersection and the fog cloaked him completely. The city was dead. He heard nothing. Daniel still had the medical files and revolver in hand, and he just stood there as if the joints in his knees had froze over. A man was running toward him. As the man passed through the fog, Daniel recognized him. It was the lawman, and he was armed.

The three had their guns out and each of them were pointed at the other. Daniel's revolver was set on the thick of the Marshal's neck. The Marshal had his sights trained between Jesse's eyes, and Jesse's shotgun faced Daniel's gut. The three men stood with anxiety's needles pricking at their fingers in a three-way standoff.

"That's my gun, lawman," Daniel muttered.

"U.S. Marsh-" O'Hara cut himself off. *His gun*? He saw the scars across Daniel's face and realized the church survivors hadn't been exaggerating about the suspect looking like a demon. "No shit."

"You got the wrong man," Jesse told the Marshal. "He is the Delamar killer; he killed my pa."

"And you're the one moving bodies on my scene, then. You're the one killing fourteen-year-old girls and shooting miners in the chest and burying em," the Marshal concluded.

"I don't got to answer to you, dammit! If you had sense you wouldn't be shooting at me. Watch me do your job and shoot this son of a bitch."

"If you let that happen, I'll shoot you down, Marshal," Daniel promised. "All three of us. Dead in the street."

"He has the right to a trial," added O'Hara.

"Like hell he does!" cursed Jesse. The shotgun quivered in his hands. "Go ahead and shoot me, then. Will that will fulfill your sense of justice and law? Long as I take this murdering coward with me, yeah you, Daniel, I got no complaints."

"That's what you would like, Jesse? Some type of way to spend the night, three people laying out in the street dead," O'Hara commented.

"I'm fine with that," Daniel threatened.

"Bull shit! I'm ending your hunt for revenge. You'll never kill the man you really want. The man you should have gunned down instead of my pa," Jesse charged.

"Captain Delamar died two years ago," Daniel replied shortly. "You ain't ending nothing, it's been over. Say goodbye and pull that trigger."

Jesse stuttered, "I-I'm fine dying here."

Two of the three in this standoff weren't all too put off by dying here, and O'Hara knew that. If he could get one of them to want to keep living, then he had a chance of walking away from this and stopping these two later in a way that didn't ensure his own death. He peered down the dull sights of the Iver Johnson and thought on how long it had been since he held a gun with the intent to kill. Each of the men was ready to fire if need be, even O'Hara.

79

───────

SAMUEL FOUND A SPOT in the bush thicket that allowed him to peer through the rifle's sights without having to stand up over the growth. He snugged the rifle against his small shoulder and held the gun steady. His father was a few yards back, trying his best to keep pace with his son who had the advantage of being able to navigate the woods silently on account of his smaller size. A patch of clearing in the forest gave Samuel a view of a buck nibbling on green thicket fifty yards west of him. The sights centered on the deer's head as Samuel held his breath and brought his finger to the trigger.

"Aim at the lungs," his father whispered, kneeling next to Samuel.

"Back up," Samuel whispered, annoyed.

"I threw off your shot?" his father asked.

"Don't worry about it." Samuel refocused on the buck.

"It'll run off."

"I'll get it in the head."

"Least aim at the neck, promised your sis some deer."

"More food if the bullet goes in the head."

"No food when you miss."

At that, Samuel pulled the trigger, and the deer collapsed out in the thicket. Samuel slung the rifle behind his back and walked over to the deer with his father behind him. When they came upon the deer, Samuel's father motioned Samuel back with his hand, worried the animal might still have some life in it and kick about.

"It's dead," Samuel said, ducking under his father's hand. He lifted up the neck of the deer, showing his father the shot bored through its brain.

"You need to start minding me. You are too quick with that trigger," his father pressed.

"Got it."

"That ain't my point, boy. You're sharp with a rifle, but you been gettin sharp with me, and that ain't how a fourteen-year-old ought to behave to his pa." His father then pinched Samuel's chin and forced his eyes up.

"Eyes on mine when I'm talking." He slapped his son's check hard enough to turn the skin red, then went on. "Smart as you are, you're dumb as hell."

They got back to the house with the deer ten minutes past four and spotted Elizabeth writing the letters of the alphabet on the bare table top. She had natural blonde curls that reached past her shoulders and down the better part of her back. Elizabeth met her father and brother excitedly, hoping they would be pleased with the characters that were now stained into the wooden face of the table. But, to Elizabeth's astonishment, her father wasn't pleased at all.

"Don't worry about it, Liz. He's been in a mood the whole day," Samuel said when their father left for the shed. She was looking at her feet. "See the deer we got?" he tried again.

"Yes," she gave.

"Still your favorite?"

"Yes," she said, clearly disinterested.

"Liz, please don't be cross with me." Samuel bent down to her eye level.

"I want to go hunting," she whined.

"Liz, you know Dad would never let that happen. You're too young, and it ain't really a thing for a lady."

"I won't say a sound. I can be real quiet."

"It ain't safe. Maybe when you're older."

"How about I show you I can do it?"

"Not until you're older."

The two bickered until Elizabeth started to cry which their father heard. Deciding on how Samuel had been acting earlier, his pa figured Samuel was being the pain and forced him out of the house till supper.

Samuel walked the path that cut down from the house and bordered the forest and farmland. It led on to a man-made clearing where a lone grave stone sat. He crouched over it resting his palm on its topside. It read, "To the Life of Catherine O'Hara, Loving Mother and Caring Wife." Samuel stayed there until the sun fell and the night chill made him shiver.

By the time he made it to the yard of the house the cold didn't bother him anymore. He paced to the front door, but stopped when he saw the rifle propped up against the porch wall. He figured his father had forgotten to lock it back in the shed, which was his usual practice. Samuel picked it up and started toward the shed, but stopped and turned to the forest instead.

An hour passed before Mr. O'Hara had finished prepping the deer. He found Elizabeth sitting in the rocker, letting it sway her back and forth as she pretended she was riding a horse. He had some meat and cut it on the counter and asked if Samuel had stumbled in yet. When Mr. Hara realized he hadn't, he asked Elizabeth to call for him outside. Mr. Hara set the table and pulled potatoes out of the storeroom and sliced them into chunks. He poured three glasses of milk, set them on the table, then seated himself. A few minutes had gone by, he got up and grabbed his coat near the door. Mr. O'Hara took his lantern from the shed and lit it. He saw the empty wall where the rifle should have been hanging and cursed. After searching for the gun, he feared that Samuel had taken the rifle out into the dark.

Elizabeth had called for Samuel again and again, moving closer to the forest border as she did. Knowing that she wasn't allowed to enter the forest by herself, especially in the dark, she hesitated at the first tree and called for her brother there. She waited there for a moment, then slowly made her way farther into the woods.

Samuel had climbed a tree and positioned himself on one of the branches with his legs wrapped over the underside. He couldn't rely on his sight with the forest being as dark as it was, so he let his mouth hang open and shut his eyes; it helped him focus on the noises around him. He imagined his father would come for him soon, holding a lamp and calling his name. Samuel could make a shot before his pa came, before he made his noisy approach and scared off any game nearby. He heard a light rustle twenty or so yards off. He scanned the forest for the source, but couldn't find it. It took another step; Samuel had a good idea now. He figured it couldn't be a full-grown deer cause of how soft its steps were. Could be a fox instead. Samuel positioned the rifle low, and after pinpointing the source, fired.

When he heard the body thud against the forest floor he scaled down the tree, paced to it, and bent down to feel what he had shot. His hand tangled in curly hair. Then he felt the smooth skin of an arm and a blood-soaked dress.

The next day another gravestone was laid beside Catherine O'Hara's, and another grave dug up by Mr. O'Hara. Samuel sat there and watched. He stayed there all day and would have spent the night there but, his father made him come in.

"OH, DON'T BE CROSS with your mother." Dara grabbed the book from the shelf as she continued. "Let me read to you."

"I know how to read," Daniel pointed out.

"Yes, you're fifteen and quick. It's more for me, Danny." Daniel came beside her and sat and Dara smiled. She opened the book, letting a twig that was keeping place fall to the wooden floor.

"Hatred is blind; rage carries you away; and he who pours out vengeance runs the risk of tasting a bitter draught." Dara changed her tone to act the voices of the characters from the "Count of Monte Cristo." She read on for the better part of an hour until someone arrived at the door.

Dara greeted Joseph Delamar with the book still in hand. Daniel knew the Captain well. He had his hand in every pot with a coin at the bottom. The Delamar Mining Company was his main source of revenue, especially after he had integrated the business with the steel industry. Recently, the Captain had begun affairs as town Mayor, which was a unanimous decision he had initially declined. Delamar commented on how he thought that story was such a "tragic" one and that he preferred "lighter tales."

Captain Delamar talked to Dara about the upcoming winter and how the town was to prepare. Dara offered tea and the Captain accepted, and when she handed him the teacup, he brushed his hand against hers.

"There are such fine gentlemen in this town. You are becoming one, Daniel," Captain Delamar announced.

"Daniel," Dara prompted her son.

"Thank you, sir," Daniel said obediently.

"Daniel, do you mind?" the Captain asked sternly. Daniel glanced at his mother.

"I think the Captain, sorry, Mayor Delamar has some personal inquiries."

"That's right," the Captain added, turning to face Dara. "Be a gentleman, would you?"

"Fetch some water, alright?" Dara asked with a crack in her voice. Daniel nodded and shook the Captain's hand before leaving.

When Daniel came back, the Captain had already left, and Daniel wasn't sure if his mother had as well. Daniel set the pail of water on the table, and the water splashed up as he did. He tried the washroom door, but it was locked and his mother called out, "A minute, Danny."

Daniel tripped on the book in the living room which was lying beside the coffee table. The tea cup that his mother had given to the Captain was also there on the floor, and its tea was spilt across the wood. Dara informed Daniel that the spill was an accident and that when the Captain came by on the next day Daniel should wake her.

The next morning the Captain returned, and Daniel answered the door.

"My mother went out," Daniel said through the slightly ajar door.

"No, she should be in," the Captain argued. "Be a gentleman and check out back."

"She went out to visit your wife Margot—she might even be at your house. Said that she needed your wife's ear. Guess you have a clear schedule."

"That right?" The Captain sneered. Daniel nodded and moved to close the door.

"How about you grab your late father's revolver and come shoot with me, since my schedule is now clear," Delamar smiled.

"My mother might worry," Daniel blurted.

"Nonsense. We will be back by supper, and she will be proud you got some practice in. Come. A gentleman wouldn't refuse."

Daniel begrudgingly accepted and told Delamar he would be out in a few minutes.

The two had been hiking for an hour before spotting a grey wolf some fifty yards out.

"Now you take that shot, Daniel," the Captain ordered.

"A revolver can't make that shot, not that far," Daniel objected.

"You can't make the shot?"

"No one could, not with this," Daniel complained as he looked down the sights which his shaking hands made difficult to line up. Delamar leaned behind Daniel to figure where he was to shoot if he fired.

"Don't aim at the head. Fire through the chest," Delamar directed.

Daniel gave the Captain a disbelieving look. "You're foolin' right? I could aim at the moon and would be just as likely to hit the damn thing."

"Fine." The Captain snatched the revolver out of Daniel's clammy hands and lined the sights to the wolf's chest and fired. The wolf wailed and snapped its head back as blood spilt down its coat.

"Watch it." Delamar brought his arm around Daniel's shoulder and held him close. The wolf ran in circles kicking up sand as it did. The beast gasped for air, but only gargled the blood that filled its windpipe. It collapsed to the ground, kicking its hind legs as it choked. "When you hit the chest, the muscles spasm, which builds pressure around its lungs and constrains them. Lungs aren't any good like that, and the only chance you would have of surviving is to breath slowly doing your best not to overexert them and take blood in. But every creature has a will to survive, and it is powerful. You can't restrain it. That will tells you to breathe. It told that creature to breathe as fast and hard as possible, that's what killed it. The best killers take advantage of that will to live and turn it against the body."

Daniel returned home minutes past supper, and Dara was waiting there for him. She slapped him when he got close.

"I told you to wake me when the Captain came!" Dara scolded.

Daniel walked past her and headed to his room where he went to bed.

When the Captain arrived the next morning, Dara was at the door and let him in. After exchanging a hollow conversation, the Captain turned to Daniel. "Be a gentleman, would you?" Dara nodded at this, and Daniel stood with a sour cringing in his stomach.

Daniel grabbed the revolver which was in his room and left. He paced east of their house into town and when he got there, he sat and pressed his boots into the dirt and waited.

JESSE STOOD BESIDE his pa in the middle of Delamar amongst the rest of the town as they congregated to face the stage where Margot stood. She had the ballots in her hand and shuffled them, aligning the edges before placing them on the podium. Joseph Delamar joined his wife on stage. In his cell behind the stage, Daniel looked out at the backs of Margot and Joseph.

"My lovely wife here has the votes that all the gentlemen of Delamar cast yesterday. This will decide if Daniel is guilty of the murder of his mother, Dara, and if he is to be hung by the neck until dead for this tragic crime." Mayor Delamar paused, looking out into the crowd. "Let's begin."

Margot read the votes from the podium one by one, calling "guilty" as she did. She kept count of the votes with each ballot she turned. "Forty-five guilty, zero innocent."

Jesse leaned close to his pa and whispered, "Why the ceremony? We all know he did it."

Margot continued with the slow process. "Four hundred and sixty-two, guilty. Zero innocent." Mayor Delamar folded his hands and bowed his head as if he were praying. Some called up from the crowd that it was "past majority vote" and to "end the count," but Delamar announced that "Daniel has a right to know the exact number of gentlemen who have determined his fate." And so, the count continued.

Finally, Margot had counted the last three votes, "Six hundred and ninety-eight, guilty. Zero, innocent. Six hundred and ninety-nine, guilty. Zero, innocent." Margot flipped the last ballot paper and read it to herself. She hesitated, then cleared her throat before continuing, "Six hundred and ninety-nine, guilty. One, innocent." Margot looked about the crowd which had become dead quiet. She quickly added, "Someone has a sense of humor," and then giggled. The crowd laughed at this, and Daniel clenched his fist.

"Who do you think that was?" Jesse asked his pa, grinning. His pa turned and walked from the crowd as Mayor Delamar announced the specifics of the hanging ceremony that would take place in three days. Jesse followed his pa then asked again, even though he was sure his pa had heard him before.

"It was me," Jesse's pa said.

Jesse laughed. "You're shitting me."

"Stop laughing. I ain't fooling," his pa snapped.

"Sure," Jesse said facetiously.

"He didn't do it. He doesn't deserve to die. Daniel was a real good kid, and if you want to laugh about that thought, you can screw off."

"Why are you sticking up for him? You owe him something?"

At this, Jesse's pa squared up to his son and grabbed him by his shirt collar. "I owe him common decency, a right to not be treated like an animal, dammit. Go ahead and condemn a man who you know nothing about, but I ain't gonna let that sin sit with me. It's a damn shame it takes one in seven hundred men to see it." Jesse's pa shoved him back, and Jesse fell to the dirt.

———————

NEITHER JESSE, DANIEL, nor O'Hara had moved within those few minutes. The fog had thickened, concealing the armed men there in the road. The three of them were set to kill each other, and O'Hara believed that on paper, that outcome wasn't all bad. He would sacrifice himself to end the killing spree that had already taken hundreds of lives. Simple counting, one loss to save many. His life was just a number. It wasn't special. Anyone else that would have been be gunned down by Daniel could now be spared. So, O'Hara didn't understand, *why am I frozen?*

"He ain't dead," O'Hara said.

Daniel sharpened his eyes on the Marshal. Jesse kept the barrel of the shotgun pointed at Daniel, trying to keep steady against his nerves.

"That Delamar guy, the one you want dead so damn bad, ain't," O'Hara forced the words out with stabbing regret.

"I got papers here that say different," Daniel claimed.

"They ain't no fact to em."

"What?" Jesse said to the Marshal in disbelief. "You're helping him?"

"I don't want any more people to die, that includes us right here."

"He was done. This was it!" Jesse shouted. "You could'a died here and so many people would have been saved. You're a coward!"

"You think you got him dead to rights, kid?" the Marshal asked Jesse, and he nodded. "You're shaking like a loose wagon wheel, he is standing there probably thinking about his breakfast."

"His gun is pointed at you, Marshal," Jesse sneered. "You fucking coward."

"You lying to me, Marshal?" Daniel asked. "You lying to save your own life?"

After pausing, O'Hara answered, "I ain't lying."

"But you are trying to save your life," Daniel pressed. The Marshal didn't look at Daniel. Jesse thought about turning the shotgun on the Marshal and killing him instead of the man who had killed his father.

"What's your move?" O'Hara asked.

Daniel twisted his gun counterclockwise in his hand and angled it upside down at Jesse's shotgun and shot Jesse's index finger off of his right hand. The severed finger rolled to the sidewalk. Jesse tried to fire back, but he instinctively pulled with the stump on his hand which made it twitch. O'Hara brought the pocket gun to face Daniel and fired, but the bullet went blindly into the dense fog as Daniel leapt onto Jesse before the Marshal could fire. The two crashed to the ground and rolled away from O'Hara in a violent scramble. O'Hara couldn't tell the two apart as they tumbled with the tails of their jackets twirling around the two. He chased after them, but only found Jesse face down in the street holding his bloody finger stump screaming in pain.

"Where did he go!" O'Hara demanded.

"Fuck you!" Jesse snapped back. O'Hara got down on his knees, grabbed Jesse by his shoulder, and turned him around. O'Hara lay his gun against the side of Jesse's head.

"Answer me!" O'Hara threatened.

"He got away, you fucking coward!"

"Rich coming from a man who kills young girls."

"I didn't have a choice! They were all dead. I went through the house looking for Daniel, and she was there with a shotgun and shot at me. I got out the way, but I..." Jesse gritted his teeth. "There weren't any options."

"Tell me what he wants!"

"He is out for revenge. He will kill all the men from Delamar who voted him guilty. And the man who accused him, the Captain."

"You better hope the court believes your shit," O'Hara said, bringing his gun to his chest and away from Jesse's head.

Jesse jolted his head to the right and when he did, the Marshal turned that way out to figure what Jesse was looking at. When the Marshal turned back, Jesse elbowed O'Hara across the skull, knocking him to the pavement. By the time O'Hara got up on his feet Jesse had retreated into the fog.

When the sun rose and the fog had cleared O'Hara paid for a room and threw his things on the bed. He went to the toilet and threw up in the bowl. His body coiled as he did, and when he was finished he laid his forehead on the cold tile and fell asleep.

DELAMAR AND THE DOCTOR had met again at the café and were halfway through their coffee when the Captain asked, "So he took it and left?"

"We can put this behind us. Everyone from Delamar can." Dr. Ryan sipped from his coffee proud to give the Captain the good news.

"I guess the ball will actually be a celebration, instead of a measure of precaution," the Captain remarked.

"Margot's ball? You didn't cancel it?"

"If I could get everyone in one place, then I knew I could stop Daniel. Hire gunmen to protect the group, hide everyone away, something to save them. I even had a train ready to transfer them to Delamar—needed multiple solutions. He already killed so many of our old friends and that tears at me."

After the two finished their breakfast Ryan gathered enough courage to ask what was on his mind.

"Out of curiosity, did Daniel shoot his mother?" Dr. Ryan was worried he had crossed a line as soon as he asked.

Delamar sighed and sipped his coffee before answering. His eyes fell to the table, and then he spoke as if he regretted the past. "Yes. He shot her." The doctor believed the Captain and decided that Daniel truly had become a lost soul. Delamar continued to stare at nothing and his face was expressionless. Ryan eased a bit closer, only to make his presence known in order to break the Captain from his thought.

"I loved that woman."

The Captain left his coffee at the table, and Ryan watched him walk away.

SHERIFF REED,

I will no longer be investigating the Delamar case. Three days from the date I send this letter I will be returning home, and my wife and I will be moving east. Please do not send any further letters.

-Samuel O'Hara

80

THE TIRES SKIDDED OVER loose sand and clay on the California wagon road when Stella pressed the brakes. The Model T stopped at a cow that was standing in the middle of the road watching Stella back through the glass. Sheriff Reed shifted in the passenger seat and opened his eyes to see the livestock out in the way.

"Guessing I woke ya?" Stella said.

Reed stretched his jaw and bent his neck. "Yeah that's alright."

Reed waved at the cow through the glass, but it didn't move. "I got some sleep because of you and that was nice."

"A nice nap." She smiled.

"I had a dream, maybe a couple. One I had before, but it ended different."

"What about?"

"No, you're just asking cause I mentioned it."

"That's a hateful thing to say."

"No one cares about other people's dreams, only their own. That's alright."

"Fine, I don't care. But I can still be an ear."

"That's sweet of you, listening to an old man." Reed lit a ciga-rette and smoked it as he continued. "The part I remember any-way, it was my father and I. My father passed years ago, and he wasn't much alive even months before he went. His body was sick; he wasn't moving less it was to the cabinet to drink. My mother was real good for staying with him then. I respect her a mighty deal for it. But in the dream, he was walking and talking and grinning again. I hadn't seen that for twenty or so years. It was nice to see when my eyes were closed. But it's painful now. Real painful. Anyway, he took me down to a train station that had just opened only ten miles off our ranch, and we were both excited to see it. He told me on the way over of how the train kept going and never tired, that even when you didn't want to move or was afraid to, it kept moving you down the tracks and across the land. That once you got on the train you didn't have no say; just look out the window and see what's out there along the tracks. You had to let it take you where it was gonna take you, even if that was to the end of the line. When we got there, we purchased seats for the train that was coming in. Everyone was older than me; I had always seen myself as a boy in this dream when I'd had it before."

Reed drank from a canteen before going on. "Anyway, we got our tickets and took our seat and waited for our train to come in. I was real excited to get on the train, but I remember just sit-ting there with my pa as he went on about the different cars and all the things that could be seen through the window pane once we got on. When it finally rolled into the station we joined the line that was gathering at the railroad car door. A man taller than my pa was taking tickets and shredding them and letting all the older folks in. When my pa gave our tickets, the man wouldn't let me on. Said they were full, said I had to wait my time, the older folks would get on first."

Reed paused again before finishing. "When I had the dream before, that is where it would end. I'd wake up right there, and that would be it. This time, it kept on, though. My father told me through the open train door that I was to get on the next train, and his train would lead the way. I told him I'd see him at the end of the line, and he nodded and the train left. When I took a seat at the station to wait for the next train I saw a bunch of the kids I knew or had met when I was growing up. I saw my wife there. She sat next to me. That shook me. The train finally came, and I gave the man the ticket and he let me on, and the train left."

When Reed finished Stella looked out to the road and the cow had left and was no longer in sight. Reed threw his cigarette out, and Stella started the car and went on down the road through the high desert heading toward Los Angeles.

A GRAYING MAN STOOD behind the counter and watched Daniel as he staggered through the door into the bank. Daniel was carrying the briefcase, and when he came near he set it up on the counter and unlatched the brass showing the teller the stacked bills.

"Making a deposit?" the teller guessed.

"I want this in gold."

The teller peered closely at a bill he removed from the case and flapped it quickly and rubbed his index finger and thumb on the bill. He looked again at the bills stacked before him.

"I don't believe we can accommodate you."

"Give me what you got."

The teller nodded before he made his way to the safe. He fetched the key from his breast pocket, opened the latch, peered inside, and counted. He locked the safe before returning.

"We only have coins in stock."

"That's what I want."

The teller took bills out from the briefcase, counted stacks of a thousand, and organized them neatly in front of him. He finished when a little more than half the briefcase had been emptied, and then he counted the stacks again. The teller took the stacks to the safe and deposited one thousand at a time, unlocking and locking the safe each trip. When he finished he took a bottle of gin out from the back with two glasses and poured four ounces for Daniel and himself. Daniel glanced at the gin. The teller drank from his glass, then placed his on the counter and wiped his lips with his sleeve.

"How are you planning on taking the gold out?"

"Put it in the case."

The teller peered at the case for a moment. "If that is how you want it."

"That's how I want it."

The teller nodded and made his way back to the safe, unlocked it, took a small, woven pouch out, and set it on the counter. The teller loosened the pouch and presented a single gold coin at a time for Daniel to approve until the bag was empty, and then the teller eased the gold back in the pouch and placed it in the suitcase. The teller drank from his glass periodically, and when all the coins had been moved to the briefcase the glass was empty. Daniel hadn't touched his glass. He left it on the counter along with a hundred-dollar bill.

O'HARA HAD HIS LUGGAGE packed on the end of the hotel bed and was washing his face with a wet rag when someone knocked at the door.

"Mr. O'Hara, if you don't plan for another night we have to kindly ask for the room back."

"And if I do plan that way?" O'Hara called back as he fixed his hair with his forefingers.

"That'd be fine, but you still owe for last night."

"How bout I walk to the bank now?"

"That'd be convenient, Mr. O'Hara. I'll be sitting down at the desk, and if I'm not just give it to the lady there."

The bank teller had sweat above his brow when O'Hara asked for his withdrawal. O'Hara noticed the glass of gin on the counter.

"Would you like it?" asked the teller when he saw the Marshal looking at the glass.

"I don't drink things I don't see poured."

"I just poured it for a gentleman who emptied out my gold stock. I ain't supposed to sell it, but the house was running low on cash and high on metal."

"I ain't gonna drink it."

On O'Hara's way back to the hotel he noticed a Model T parked at the curb with a pretty, curly-headed woman inside reading a paper. O'Hara gave the woman another look and then had to look again.

"Stella! What the hell are you doing here?" O'Hara scolded. Stella's face went white as her body started up from shock.

"Don't shake me like that! Jesus, Sammy!"

"Whose car is this?"

"Sheriff Reed's. He had some real important thing to tell you."

"It better be the house burned down and he was returning you to me."

"Returning?" Stella rolled her eyes up.

"You knew that ain't what I meant by it. Where is the Sheriff?" Stella pointed behind her at the Sheriff walking up to the car. Reed explained why he had come and how Stella had forced her way onto his trip. He began to tell the Marshal about what Maryanne had said, but O'Hara cut him off.

"You're a bit late. Ran into him last night." O'Hara watched people passing by on the other side of the street.

"I was worried that you'd shot him instead."

"It crossed my mind."

"Jesse was a good kid, always been."

"Things ain't been like they always been."

"That's a truth that is more obvious now than in all my years working as Sheriff." Reed looked O'Hara in the eye for a moment before O'Hara diverted his gaze back to watching the street. Reed could tell the Marshal was stalling about something, so the Sheriff waited for the man to speak.

"Sheriff, I sent you a letter, and when you get it just read it and let that be it." Reed pursed his lips when the Marshal said this, then lit a cigarette and offered it to O'Hara.

O'Hara waved the cigarette away, and the two just stood as the street made its noise around them. Reed let the stick fall from his hand and smothered it with the front of his boot.

"I ain't gonna open that letter." Reed spat into the gutter and walked off leaving O'Hara behind.

SAMUEL AWOKE IN THE hotel. He checked on Stella, who seemed to be sleeping well. He stared up at the ceiling. It was a white drywall that didn't have anything worth looking at, but he still looked and did so for a while. Samuel stepped out of bed and made his way to the washroom, lit the bulb, and studied himself in the mirror. He was sweating. He cupped water in his hands and brought it to his face and scrubbed.

"Sammy," Stella said while yawning. "What's the matter?" she continued.

Samuel blew out the light and then walked to the bed and sat at its foot. Stella sat up and caressed his back with her nails.

"You're drenched." Stella got out of bed and grabbed the towel from the washroom, soaked it in water, and then washed Samuel's back. Samuel arched his back slightly when the chilled water pressed against his neck. She placed her lips on his cheek and kissed him. Samuel interlaced his fingers and pressed his forehead against his knuckles. His elbows rested on his knees. Samuel closed his eyes.

"She's proud of you." Stella laid back down. "She's smiling. Can't you feel it?"

Samuel prayed. He saw Elizabeth; he always did when he shut his eyes like this to think. She stood barefoot beside a redwood that had no bark. Dried pine needles covered the earth. The needles poked up between the crevices of her toes. Elizabeth placed her palm against the redwood. "It has got no skin." The leaves of the tree browned and fell from its fragile branches and blanketed over the pine needles. "Sammy." Elizabeth looked at the tree and it fell when she did.

Stella lay awake.

"I got to see this through," Samuel finally spoke. Stella set her hand on his side to let him know she had heard him, and then he fell back into bed beside his wife.

"I love you, Sammy, and I always will." Stella waited for Samuel to fall asleep before shutting her eyes.

WHEN THE SUN WAS SETTING Reed found a Sheriff station on the west side of Los Angeles. He made his way to a local deputy who didn't seem all too busy and asked if he could spare a few minutes.

"Yeah, maybe, what about?" the Deputy asked, slightly annoyed.

"I was wondering if you had any incidents last night?"

"It's Los Angeles. We always got incidents."

"Any shootouts?"

"Look, I'd like to help ya out, but tonight is a busy night. Why don't you come in tomorrow?"

"I'm sure you're working hard."

"Yeah, Delamar is having this birthday celebration for his wife tonight and we are expecting drunks and the type of trouble drunks stir up."

"Delamar?"

"Sir, I don't have any time to be chatting right now. Come on in when it's the morning."

"That's alright, but where should I go to keep away from the drunks?"

"Delamar's manor is five blocks north, so anywhere but there."

"Thank you kindly." Reed tipped his hat and left.

It didn't take Reed all too long to find the Delamar manor; he went north five blocks like the deputy had said then followed the first dressed couple he saw. They led him to the front gate of the manor, where Reed decided it'd be best if he stopped there and kept a look out. The manor was a pure white, as if it had been painted in a fresh coat every morning. It had two grand columns that were thicker than Sequoia trees, and the front door rose high enough Reed imagined you could ride through them on horseback. A doorman took names from a list and let the guests in accordingly.

Reed watched guests enter until he saw Jesse, who had a white cloth wrapped around his right hand. After talking to the doorman, who saw Jesse's name on the list, Jesse stepped through that grand doorway. Reed waited for the walkway up to the manor to be empty, save the doorman, before making his way over.

"Name?"

"I don't imagine I'm on the list."

"What's your name?" the doorman pressed.

"Lionel Reed."

The doorman scanned through his list. He shook his head as he did.

"The man you just let in, Jesse, why?"

"He was on the list."

"Why's that?"

"You're on the list if you're from Delamar. Some type of reunion."

Reed scratched his forehead, grimacing, before he showed the doorman his badge. "Jesse's got other plans tonight."

"This is private land, Sheriff."

"I understand that you have to keep things peachy. With him in there that won't happen."

"I don't want some bonanza."

"I'll get him out quietly, no fuss."

The doorman reluctantly agreed and shut the door after Reed entered.

The party was overly festive for the Sheriff's taste. He thought half the people there would do themselves some good if they sat for a moment and drank a bit of water. In a crowd of drunks, a sober person sticks out like a virgin in a brothel, and the Sheriff reasoned that was why he was able to spot Jesse as quickly as he did. Jesse noticed Reed immediately as well, and after they stared at each other, Reed nodded to the side, and Jesse understood his signal to meet him in the hall.

Jesse had beat the Sheriff to the semi-private hall and had his shotgun pointed at the Sheriff as he rounded the corner.

"I like ya, Reed, but I know why you're here and I ain't going to oblige," Jesse started.

Reed didn't go for his gun. "Jesse, let's go home. They hadn't gotten to a proper burial for your pa yet. Your father would want you to be there to bless his place in the earth."

Jesse reddened and tears stung his cheeks. "Don't! I know what you're on about. The next funeral I will be attending is Daniel's."

"I'm going to take my revolver out, and you are going to put that shotgun down. Then we can ride back. If you have any other plans, then go ahead and shoot me." Reed folded his coat back as he reached for his gun.

"Don't! Christ, Reed, I will shoot, I swear it—you're making me do this!" Jesse's tears ran. He raised the shotgun to chest level.

The two were interrupted by someone who shouted from the main ballroom, "Gold! It's gold!"

Dr. Ryan pushed through the front door and hurried out of the manor and down the entrance into the street. He didn't notice the doorman who was laid out on the porch soaked in blood. Once Ryan was gone, Daniel came around from the back of the yard with a chain and fastened it around the front door, locking it from the outside.

BY THE TIME THE MARSHAL had heard about what had occurred at the Delamar manor and made his way to the outlying gate of the estate, an investigation was already underway. He had to shift through a group of bystanders to get to the gate entrance where a local policeman was keeping folks controlled as best he could. The policeman shooed the Marshal back before O'Hara could explain, which didn't rub O'Hara the right way.

"I'm a Marshal," O'Hara snapped.

"You got a badge?"

The Marshal shoved his badge into the Sheriff's chest and went on through the gate.

The door had blood smeared on the knocker that trailed off to a body a few feet out from the entrance. The metal chain had been cut from the door and was lying there on the porch. The Marshal bent his fingers around the door's side and opened it cautiously, as if he was a lion's cage. He stared through the manor's entryway at the ball floor. His boots were loud on the marble, the acoustics of the room making the noise vibrant and powerful.

Bodies weren't littered about like they had been at the church. Instead they were organized on the floor with pools of blood connecting them all. There were some bodies scattered about, but three large groups stuck out to the Marshal. They were at the exits, piled over one another. "They were trying to flee, but must have gotten bottlenecked and shot. In trying to escape, they made themselves easier to kill, all being crammed in the same spots," the Marshal thought.

O'Hara bent down and looked at the face of a man who had something in his hand. O'Hara opened the body's cold hand and took a gold coin out from its grasp. He spun the coin slowly between his fingers and then let it fall on the ground. O'Hara stood up and scanned the ballroom floor. O'Hara couldn't count all the gold he saw, and it was at that point he came to know how close he was to a coincidence yesterday.

It took the Marshal about an hour to count all the bodies in the ballroom, which summed to fifty-five gentlemen. "This is what one night off looks like." O'Hara found a blood trail that led out back behind the stage where the band would play, and he followed it though the back rooms of the manor. The tracks were muddled with dirt and footprints and parted in the kitchen where one trail went back toward the ballroom. O'Hara believed this was Daniel's, he couldn't think of anyone else who want to return to the ballroom.

The trail led him to a narrow hall where an older man lay face down. His shirt was stained with blood which had poured out there on onto the floor, but the carpet was a dim red so the Marshal wasn't all too sure how much the man had bled. The body was sprawled out in a way that it was impossible not to step over it if you wanted to get across the hall. This investigation had been going on for the better part of the day, and no one had had the decency to roll the body to the side. Instead they stepped over it, like anything else out on the ground. From then on, the Marshal was of the opinion that all the other lawmen there were just a bunch of cowboys.

When O'Hara knelt down to move the body he spotted a golden object about ten paces out and the Marshal thought it was a coin, but it was a shotgun cartridge, and it had an "H" engraved on the side. O'Hara went back to the body and rolled it to its back and saw Reed's face. Sheriff Reed had been shot in his lower side by a shotgun and had been dead for hours. O'Hara grimaced, and then closed Reed's eyes.

25

DR. RYAN WIPED HIS palms against the tails of his suit jacket, but didn't help. His hands were sweating from the inside out. He hesitated before knocking. The door was at the end of the hall, and that made the doctor's approach all that much tougher. When he did knock, Delamar opened it immediately.

"Go seat yourself."

The doctor paused before trudging in and saw the round table in the corner with two wooden chairs. A revolver was laid out in front of one chair, while a fresh copy of the Los Angeles Times was at the other. The doctor sat in front of the latter.

Delamar glared until the doctor looked back.

"Do you remember being a child?" asked Delamar.

The doctor started up from his seat, but sat back when Delamar ordered him to stay with his open palm.

"What about eating with your family?"

"Yes."

"Good, one should remember their family meals. There is a system in place that a child either doesn't notice or doesn't value. Each family member has a role in the house to ensure that a meal and shelter can be shared for that night and the next. The family serves the house, which then protects that family. When

I was Captain of the Queen's vessel there was a system as well, individuals all doing their part to help the whole. It's because I not only understand this, but more so that I believe in the system, that I am often at the head of them."

As Delamar spoke, he prepared himself a glass of neat whiskey. The doctor watched how the Captain raised the glass to eye level when he poured.

He downed half the whiskey without a grimace. "Name me a system, so I know you and I are within understanding."

Ryan cleared his throat. "Well, the organ systems are—"

"Yes!" Delamar spoke over Ryan excitedly. "Of course the doctor would think of the organs, the parts, and the body, the whole." Delamar smiled. "The stomach has to digest food. The heart pumps the blood. All for the body—so what am I?"

"Out of the organ system?"

Delamar nodded.

"You would be the body."

Delamar's enthused expression cut out. "What about in the household."

"You would be the house that protects the family."

Delamar finished his whiskey, gave the doctor's answer a nod, and then pitched the glass into the wall above the doctor where it shattered, raining shards onto the table.

Delamar barked down at the doctor. "I am the brain! I am the father! I am the only part of the system that has the cognitive ability to fear the virus, the robber, the system's end, and when that end comes, I am the one who recognizes that the only part at fault is myself! The other parts will die off in fear, but I already felt that fear, so I die with guilt. Your job in our system was to buy Daniel. Instead, you gave the robber our meal, and then he shot us at the table!"

Delamar sat at the other end of the table, took up the pistol, and drove the barrel into the face of the table. "On my ship, when a member of the system hurt the system, I put them on the plank, took two muskets, and shot a hole through each foot!" Delamar fired the revolver, slid it across the table, and then fired again. The doctor winced at the sound. Splinters cratered around the entry points of each bullet on the table's face.

"Then I told them to *crawl* the plank! And every member of our system watched the expatriate crawl and leave its blood on the wood, then fall into the waves and wait for a beast with three rows of teeth to eat them foot to head. So when I asked you to seat yourself, do you think you should have sat where you are with a paper in front of you, or should you have sat here and taken this pistol and shot Daniel in the street?"

Delamar let the gun clatter onto the table when he stood and waited for the doctor to get up and take his seat. When he did, Delamar sat, opened the paper, folded it to a particular page, and slid it in front of the doctor. The text on the page read, "Horror Manor; A Festive Night Turned Deadly."

"Fifty-five gentlemen died last night, the same night I was set to tell them we did not have to worry anymore, that I had played the role of the father and protected us." The anger had left the Captain; instead, he spoke with regret.

"I'm sorry," the doctor muttered, while his lip quivered involuntarily.

Delamar softened his voice. "The lives lost... We can't let the whole die, despite how small it has become. Take redemption, doctor."

Ryan hesitated, feeling skittish and spooked. "I'll take it."

"I have arranged transportation from here to Delamar. Everyone in Los Angeles will know about this train, so we can ensure all the survivors of our system will be on that train. But Daniel will also know. You have to get on that train; it will be the 7:00 am to Mohave. At that stop, you will lead them onto the Southern Pacific Railroad where you will take another train to Needles, and I will be waiting there. Do you understand?"

The doctor wiped his face with his sleeve and agreed.

"Take that gun with you. Protect the whole."

The doctor found a place for the pistol in his suit, and then patted that spot as if to check if it had disappeared within those few seconds.

O'HARA SAT BESIDE HIS wife at the foot of the hotel bed and they both looked straight ahead. Stella used a hand cloth to wipe her eyes dry, but she cried again just after. She clenched the cloth in her hand, and her tears drizzled out from her chin onto the back of her hand. She shook her head and dried her face, and Samuel wrapped his arm around her shoulder and held her.

"How do I tell his wife?" Stella whimpered.

"Don't think of it."

"I'm going to tell her."

A speaker phone blared on the top of a police-outfitted Model T as it rolled down the street at walking speed.

"This is the third time it's been round," Stella cautioned.

"It ain't honest."

The speaker phone called for any Delamar survivors to congregate at the downtown train station at 6:45 am. It continued on with specifics of Captain Delamar's plan to safeguard against the walking evil.

"A train just ain't safe," Stella said.

"I'm boarding that train."

"I know. You have to. It's just, have you been thinking like I have been?"

"Get on with it."

"This ain't gonna ring out, Sammy."

"Yeah."

"Maybe I'm saying things you already thought. I know I have before. You're too sweet to say nothing, but I gotta say it."

"You got a softer voice than the one in my head."

"It's bait, or a donkey-brained plan. Imagine the killer has heard this, all the people he wants dead, all practically in the same room, a moving room that no one can leave and everyone knows where it's going. What more could the killer want? It's an invitation for him to finish what he started."

"Tell me what to do."

Stella thought for a moment, before she shook her head and cried. "You gotta get on that train."

Samuel hugged Stella firmly. "I'm going to start in the back of the train and clear each car as I move to the front. I will order everyone to squeeze into the two tail cars and once I reach the front, move back and detach the last cars. If Daniel is in the train, I'll shoot him. If he has a trap set down the tracks, I'll detach the tail cars. I won't have any more good people killed."

DANIEL LEFT THE MINING camp with ten thousand dollars' worth of dynamite sticks which he had paid twice that for in a saddle bag that he had slung over his shoulder that could stretched the length of his back. When morning was a few hours away, Daniel found the train station where the 7:00 am to Mohave was to depart from. The train had five seat cars and even though it was dark, Daniel could make out the painting on the side of a car that read, "Golden State Limited." There wasn't a soul in sight.

Daniel tried the five seat cars, but they were locked, and Daniel left it at that. The tow car door opened into the engine room, which was organized in a fashion where two people were meant to conduct the train. A couple containers of coal were stacked near the furnace next to a tool-crate. Daniel dragged the tool-crate out of the train and into the wilderness a hundred yards out. He dumped the tools behind a manzanita bush and scattered the pile in the sand. He carried the crate back and placed it near the others, returning it to the original position, then crouched in it to confirm if he would fit. He did, and it wasn't all that uncomfortable, either.

At the tail car, Daniel lay on his back and wormed his way under the rails and wheels with the bag of dynamite. He strapped the sticks to the underside of the car, wired a timer to the explosives, and set it for six hours from then. The saddle bag still had a quarter of the dynamite left when Daniel finished. After a spell, he decided to place the extra sticks under the fourth seat car. When he was satisfied, he gave a last look at the train, then climbed into the crate he had prepared for himself.

IT WAS TEN PAST SEVEN when the train departed. The train had five cars and had "Golden State Limited" painted in gold on both sides of each car with a brownish-red color as the foreground that had originally been painted bright red, but had been darkened and weathered by wind and sand. It was lined with windows large enough for the Marshal to fit his head through and had a silver metal streak under the pane. There wasn't a car with an empty seat, and each chair car had about twenty seats to them. The Marshal watched out the window waiting till he couldn't see the city anymore and then got up and looked about the back car as a whole. He shifted his jacket to reveal the Marshal badge that was pinned to his shirt.

"Now I'm gonna have to ask for no one to leave this car. It'll get cozy, but you all stay put." The Marshal searched for any objections in the car; a toddler smiled at him and he nodded at the boy. O'Hara forced the door to the gangway open and let it shut behind him. He stood out on the platform and felt the ramp shift and shake beneath his feet. The air was moist. O'Hara felt it on his lips.

Jesse peered out the back window and saw the Marshal enter the car behind him. Jesse was in the middle car trading looks over his shoulders between the front and back windows. He didn't think he would see the Marshal after that night, but here he was one car back, and Jesse wasn't all that excited about it neither. The Marshal had his hand in his jacket pocket, and Jesse knew that it was gripped around some kind of pistol. Jesse scrambled to the front of the middle car and peered out that window into the next car, but he didn't see anything. The whole passenger car was staring at Jesse, nervous about the suspicious behavior. Jesse snatched a shotgun out from inside his jacket with his left hand and threatened the car with it. The barrel had been sawed off, and it wasn't even the length of his arm.

A woman stared at his right hand, deformed by the missing index finger.

"Everyone needs to keep quiet in here. Fact is, if ya talk," Jesse rocked the shotgun with his fingers, "he's gonna talk back."

The Marshal helped the last person out of the fourth car, across the gangway, and into the fifth car where it was already cramped. O'Hara paced back through the empty fourth car and onto the connecting ramp from the fourth to the third. He stopped to feel the road beneath him again. He inspected the link and pin coupling beneath him, then the passenger car in front of him. The faces were tense. No one was speaking, and they all had a look as if they were trying their best not to be noticed. O'Hara spotted one man who was watching the door. His eyes focused near the floor of the door. O'Hara gripped the door handle and turned it slightly for it to make a noise and waited. O'Hara slid his hand into his suit pocket and pointed the hidden revolver at the window ahead. A loud burst shattered the window and the glass shards sprayed over O'Hara, forcing him to cover his face. As O'Hara moved his hand, Jesse had the shotgun out on the ledge of the broken window leveled point blank at the Marshal's chest. O'Hara fired at Jesse, forcing him to duck under the door and misplace his second pellet shot which flew out to the sky. By the time Jesse reloaded, O'Hara was bunkered to the right of the door inside the fourth car.

When coal needed to be repositioned on the furnace the coal shoveler opened the tool crate, and Daniel shot him in the chest. The conductor turned toward the sound, and Daniel sat up with his back against the wood and the pocket gun set on the conductor's chest.

"I ain't gonna kill you," Daniel told him.

The conductor's eyes trailed toward the coal shoveler's body.

"I need this train to get to Delamar," Daniel said.

"That's where it's going at the end."

"Throw any pieces you have out."

The conductor eased out the revolver he had in his holster and threw it out from the train. He then took up the coach gun that was resting under the conductor's chair and did the same with it. Daniel pointed his barrel at the dead shoveler, and the conductor slid the pistol out of the dead man's pocket and tossed it out.

"Stay up here and don't mind any racket in the back," Daniel ordered before making his way into the first car.

His stomach curled and soured as he looked at each face in the front chair car. His brain was screaming, punishing itself for being so stupid. The tow car whistled, and people in the car with Daniel protected their ears from the sharp sound. A thirteen-year-old girl whined about the shrieking, then asked her pa if they could move to the second car. The man sitting next to Daniel tucked the crown of his hat down past his eyes and leaned back. Daniel scanned every face in the car with him, and each one was new to him. Daniel's gut told him to check each car to look for the Delamar men, but Daniel knew that was blind hope. There wasn't anybody from Delamar on this train. He knew that.

Daniel peered through the back door into the second car. Andrew Ryan was sitting with his front facing Daniel, and when the doctor saw Daniel through the glass, he turned cold. Daniel walked over the gangway into the second chair car and stood above the doctor who had a revolver across his lap shaking in his moist hand.

"You know?" the doctor quivered.

"I know now."

"And then?"

"I need to get to the back."

"You gonna kill these people?"

"No."

The doctor looked at his lap. He wept and watched his tears splash against the barrel. "Daniel, I couldn't had done nothing back then. With the Captain."

Daniel drew and lined his barrel at the doctor's forehead.

"You can pull that trigger, but you didn't kill me Daniel."

Daniel's thumb set the hammer.

"The Captain ordered me here. I was put out to water."

A gun fired from a distance.

"He killed me."

The doctor closed his eyes. Daniel lifted the Iver Johnson from the doctor, and then paced to the back window of the second car. Ryan opened his eyes and turned to see Daniel's back. No one in the car moved; they sat too afraid. Daniel stopped at the window, and despite the glare on the glass, he could see Jesse's leg sticking out from behind a passenger chair. The doctor counted to three in his head, then stumbled to his feet bouncing the revolver up so that the barrel aimed at Daniel's back. Daniel, using the reflection in the window as a reference, swiveled his arm behind his back and shot Ryan through the throat. The doctor stumbled to the floor and applied pressure to his throat. Blood seeped up between the crevices of his boney hand, then pooled over the knuckles and spilled out down his forearms onto the train floor. The doctor breathed in the blood as it filled his lungs, suffocating him as if he was drowning.

Daniel raised his revolver above his head and shouted, "Get to the front car!"

The passengers of the second car were petrified. Daniel grabbed a teenager up by the shoulder pad of his coat and shoved him toward the front of the car, threatening him with the barrel. "Now!" Daniel ordered.

Once the car was empty, save for Ryan's body, Daniel looked toward the rear car and spotted Jesse and the lawman shooting at each other. Daniel fired out the window of the front of the third car and called out to Jesse.

"Let me through to the back!"

Jesse popped his head out from cover and let off a pellet round at Daniel. Daniel slid behind the train walls as the pellets sparked against the metal exterior. O'Hara pivoted his head and spotted Daniel's shoulder protruding out from the wall's cover. He lined the sights at Daniel, but when he did, Jesse bent his hand over the window with the shotgun and fired blindly at the Marshal. This threw off O'Hara's aim and forced him to his knees to avoid pellets which lit up against the metal roof above. Hot particles showered down onto O'Hara. Daniel took this as his chance to fire at Jesse, who was shuffling shells into the shotgun, but when Daniel eased out from cover, the Marshal was ready and fired. The bullet tore through the top of Daniel's shoulder, and he cursed as he let his back slam against the cover.

"Jesse!" Daniel tried again.

"Let me see that face!"

"They are gonna die! These people aren't from Delamar."

Jesse laughed as he emptied the shotgun, and the pellets clattered against the inner train wall.

"This is a U.S. Marshal. Put your firearms down and lay on the ground." No response. As it was, the Marshal knew he was pinned. He figured the front two cars were stacked full with bodies already. O'Hara could detach now and save what he had, but going out on that gangway was a fast way to eat bullets.

Blood curled down Daniel's back soaking through to his coat. He rose swiftly, but as he did, the pain in his shoulder forced him to the ground.

O'Hara slid the door open and crawled onto the gangway, keeping as low as possible. He got his hand underneath the metal path and gripped the coupling's latch. It wouldn't budge. Sweat beaded from his forehead, and after trailing past his eyebrows, blurred his vision. O'Hara needed to detach now, but the latch was stiff and the shaking ramp made getting a tight hold difficult. His time was up. The door slid open in front of him, and Jesse leaned over with the shotgun, its barrel just about touching the Marshal's forehead. O'Hara gritted his teeth and brought his revolver forward as a reflex.

The fifth car flew up from the tracks with fire beneath it as the explosives detonated, ripping the car apart in the air, flinging the pieces of train about. The flame bellowed through into the fourth car as it folded in two. Jesse had a split glimpse of the Marshal being flung into the air then disappearing into the fire and debris.

The gangway between the third and fourth car tore the door and the back wall apart, and Jesse scrambled forward, but was knocked sideways from the force and rolled toward the contorted opening. He caught a protruding piece of steel which cut his hand as he hung on. When he slipped farther down he let go of the shotgun to grab the bent metal with both hands, letting his gun roll off the train into the desert sand as he yanked himself back onto the train. Jesse stared at the rubble as the front half the train continued along the tracks.

Daniel's pocket gun tapped against the back of Jesse's head.

"Do it!" Jesse called.

"All you had to do was let me through. The dynamite could have been defused. Your stubbornness killed those people." Daniel explained with a defeated air about him.

"You killed them—you been killing people, and they didn't deserve none of what you did to em."

"The people I killed, had a debt."

"None of them owed you shit. You're just a crybaby who is mad he got put in the corner. We voted you guilty cause you're guilty."

"The Captain framed me, and no one was strong enough to fight for what was right."

"The Captain is a mean man. A mean, son-of-a-bitch. But he loved our town. We were a family, his family."

"I imagined you would beg."

"I got no guilt. Six-hundred and ninety-nine knew what a sick fuck you are. Me included. My father was the only moron out of 700 who let his heart get in front of his mind and vote you innocent. You talk about debt, but you owe my father; you owe me my father!" Jesse shut his eyes. "Do it!"

Daniel studied the desert sand beside the train then lifted his foot and pushed Jesse from the ledge with the bottom of his boot. Jesse rolled against the tracks when he hit the ground and then lay in the sand as he watched the train shrink in the distance.

JOSEPH DELAMAR FIT the pick under one of the wooden planks and pulled back on the pick to splinter the wood from the nails. With him were twenty-two men; all had tools and worked at ripping the railroad tracks up from the clay. After twenty yards of railroad had been dismantled and thrown to the side, Delamar led the group about a hundred yards back from the tracks where they waited for the train to come in.

A couple men argued that there might be other survivors on the train, that the trap would injure too many innocent people.

Delamar addressed this sharply, "Daniel has already killed six-hundred plus. That is more life than some farmers take in cattle. God bless whoever got on that train, but it's too late for remorse. We needed to be here to ensure Daniel failed, send a message to society that fantastical plots of revenge and quests of mass vengeance never materialize. My conscience is scratching at the inside of my skin, too, but this is the only way Daniel can be stopped. God will pardon us, and if he doesn't I will rot in Hell believing I gave the best of me to earth."

When the train came, its torn and bent metal screeched as if it was wailing out in pain. Delamar readied the men and they approached the train. It crashed against the clay earth where track had once lay and fell to its side, skidding against the sand till it stopped silently.

24

DANIEL DIDN'T NEED to open his eyes to know where he was. When you wake up in your bed, you know where you are. Daniel knew where he was. The feeling hadn't changed. The water still dripped. The cold floor still clung to his back. It still felt like his grave.

"Welcome home," Margot said from outside the bars.

She struck cords of hate and terror through Daniel. He bolted up and scooted back to the far wall, instinctively reaching for his holster but, it was empty.

"You really sucked the life out of my party." Margot leaned her forehead against two bars and grasped them with her hands.

"Go to Hell!"

"The fare's too high"

"A lady like yourself, who's done the things you've done... I'll buy you that ticket to Hell."

"Well, you already bought your mothers."

Daniel ran at Margot with his hand out to grab her by the dress and bash her head against the bars till her eyeballs rattled in her skull, but she stepped back beyond his reach. The dried blood on his shoulder cracked with the reopening of his wound. His whole body was bruised, and his head was numb.

"My husband will hang you tomorrow. I think that's soft." She looked at Daniel with her chin raised and her eyes edged down. "Don't count on a miraculous escape again."

When Margot was halfway up the stairs, she crept back down and saw Daniel trying to force the lock.

"How *did* you escape?"

Daniel shook the lock harder while keeping his eyes on Margot's.

THE LIVING ROOM WAS simple enough. It had one couch in front of a tan coffee table, enough room for two to sit by each other's side. The interior was dated, but had been kept up nicely, other than awkward to reach spaces where dust had gathered.

Stella was quivering on the couch. She had been crying since she had arrived and was just now able to hold her sobs. But when Stella brought the tea cup to her mouth, she had to set it back on the table because the tears started again.

"I told him it wasn't going to ring out." She sobbed as she went on. "I knew this man was a monster—something dangerous. And out of all the cases he went on, this had to be the one. Men have to act so goddamn noble, and I don't know what for."

"Dear, I have no interest in a man that lacks resolve," an older lady comforted Stella from the kitchen.

"How are you so composed about this? I envy that, ma'am. I knew him for a bit over a month, and I can't keep my emotions together."

"I would never expect a lady carrying a child that late to keep herself together. That'd be unfair." Reed's widowed wife, Nancy, came into the living room and sat beside Stella.

"It would be fair if you blamed us," Stella whispered.

Nancy scoffed at that idea. "My husband talked to me about the Marshal every day. When he was here, he was obsessing about the case, writing your husband about any detail. I could tell he wanted to be there."

"But he went out and got himself killed."

"One certainty is that we will all die. But how and when, the life you carved out for yourself decides that. Men die from drink, men die from stupidity, and men die from wanting what ain't theirs. Reed didn't go too early, and he didn't let something like greed take him. That is something I am proud of. He left in good character. But I wouldn't be able to argue that he didn't die from stupidity."

She smiled, and so did Stella.

"He died trying to protect, like a shield crumbling after countless blows. And when I think on it, there is no better ticket up to our Lord than a selfless act like that."

"You won't miss him?"

"I already do. Makes me weak. But he didn't turn rotten before he died. He left his best on the table."

The women spent the day talking about Reed and the many different turns and sights he had had through life. And when night fell, and Stella was about to make her way on back to the house, they hugged and Stella thought they were a lot like sisters.

―――――――――――

JESSE WALKED ALONG the tracks with a gimpy foot and a face that had been burned by the sun. His hands were caked with dried blood and grains of sand that had been lodged into his skin from the fall.

When he got to the derailed train, he stood and just looked at the mess for a while. Two of the passenger cars had tipped to their side, partially buried into the top layer sand. After searching through the wreckage, he found a couple of bodies that hadn't been dead for long, one being the doctor whom he recognized. The doctor was inside one of the cars that laid on its end. Jesse crouched into the car and maneuvered over the seats that now acted as the floor. His boots cracked against the few window fragments that had survived. Beside the doctor was the medical bag, and Jesse took it up and rummaged through the compartments, finding an extensive selection of medical tools including a stitching kit and tongs. He put the alcohol and bandages to the side, set the bag on the underside of the seat, then dabbed and covered his wounds. When the injures stopped bleeding, Jesse continued out of the car to look at the bodies, turning them over thinking that one might be Daniel, to no such luck. There was a canteen near the outside of the second car, and Jesse was hopeful. He raised it, empty. Something pulled at his arm, and then the sound of the shot came. His arm felt wet. Another bullet tugged on his shoulder, and Jesse sprinted behind the side of one of the cars. He sat unarmed, bleeding, and panting.

The Iver Johnson's sights were steady as O'Hara limped along the tracks. His coat was partly burned off, and second-degree burns covered his back. O'Hara shot at Jesse from forty yards out from the cars. The walk alone was a great task for the Marshal. His wounds were chafing against one another as he moved and O'Hara was sweating and shaking from the pain. He walked a wide circle around the car that he had seen Jesse duck behind, making sure he kept a safe distance. O'Hara didn't want to make the same mistake in Los Angeles. Jesse stared at the Marshal rounding the side of the train looking as though this was his first stop after leaving Hell. O'Hara had Jesse's sawed-off in one hand and the Iver Johnson in the other pointed at Jesse.

"How are you walking?"

"Real fine way to ruin a gun." O'Hara shook the sawed-off.

"You're the Marshal who don't die."

"I ordered you to lay down with your piece thrown off, but you didn't. You came close to shooting me. Now I'm closer."

"Me taking orders? From a fucking coward like you?"

"Yeah, you don't respect law. Even from old-timers." The Marshal tossed the sawed-off to the ground between them, letting the "H" marked shells bounce and roll about.

"Hey, hold on, I didn't kill Reed."

O'Hara fired a round that cut off the top of Jesse's ear. Jesse wailed and held the bit of ear that was left as blood curled round the back of his neck.

"No one's buying your bullshit," O'Hara said, maintaining his calm demeanor.

"I ain't got to answer to a coward like you!"

"I don't expect a deaf man to answer." The Marshal traced the barrel to Jesse's other ear.

"I didn't have a choice! Reed was gunning for me!"

"Reed was looking out for you! He held that you were a good kid, told me to save my bullets if I saw you."

"It's your fault Reed is dead! He would still be alive, along with them people at the ball and them ones here, but you... You had to save yourself and tell Daniel the Captain wasn't dead. Us three could have died that day instead of the hundreds that are dead now! You stopped that. You couldn't make the sacrifice I was willing to! You're supposed to be a lawman. So how is it that a nobody like me was willing to do what you weren't?"

"You and I wouldn't have any business with each other if you weren't anybody, but you're a criminal."

"You're just a fucking coward!"

"I can't argue that. I have been terrified, and it's people that are scaring me. I am a coward who fears leaving his wife and unborn child to a world where men like you and Daniel take good blood from people just to fulfill your own objectives. And you are a fool if you don't fear living with people like yourself."

Jesse wanted to yell, but he didn't. "I'm sorry! I liked Reed just fine, but he was gonna take me in and I can't have that, not till I get what Daniel owes me. There was no other way about it."

O'Hara paused before he asked, "At what point is a debt less expensive to forgive?"

"I ain't doing this for only me. I met a miner kid before he died. I buried him. His jaw was all cocked back wrong, but I could see in him something more than fear. More than a fear of dying. It was guilt. He had guilt in him, and seeing him with that guilt cut me. If I don't shoot Daniel down, I'm bound to die with that same guilt. I won't die with guilt, no matter the cost."

"You kneel in front me saying you have no guilt. No guilt for Reed, no guilt for that young woman on the Higgans' ranch. Guilt is all you should be. Fact, if you really ain't feeling remorse for your crimes, then I will blow out your knees and leave you here to starve."

Jesse's voice cracked. "All any of us are, are collectors of guilt. Every man who can't do perfect lives with his stock of mistakes. It's more than I can carry. Forgive me, Marshal." Jesse bent his neck up to look at the transparent sky. "Forgive me, Reed, but I won't stop till he is dead. I won't stop till that guilt is gone."

Suddenly the Marshal's feet bent under his weight, making him stumble. It took him a deal of effort to keep steady, his head kept wanting to fall back. He folded the front of his coat over the cut and gripped a quarter-wide bar of metal that was sticking out from his gut. He pressed along the side of it where it went into his skin, and he grunted in pain.

"That's a mean piece of shrapnel you got in you."

O'Hara's head glided back before he brought it forward again. Then he collapsed to his knees.

"The last Marshal, that's what I'll remember you as."

O'Hara coughed, and blood sprayed out onto the sand. It nearly dried before he was able to raise his pistol. "Okay, cowboy, my finger will pull before my life does."

"There was a doctor on this train."

O'Hara's finger shifted from guard to trigger.

"You're not thinking. I used a medicine case to help me up pretty good. I might feel inclined to use it and fix you up, clean up that mess you got there." Jesse clarified.

"Why would you?"

"For my life, your life."

"Bullshit, you'll spit on my body and laugh."

"My hands are already red." Jesse raised his open hands, which were drenched in blood.

O'Hara shook his head. "Last words?"

Jesse gulped. "Do what you have to, Marshal."

The pocket gun shook in O'Hara's hand until he couldn't hold on anymore, and he fainted. Jesse watched him lay in the dirt till Jesse was confident the Marshal wasn't coming to again. Then Jesse stood up and spat on the dirt.

THE CAPTAIN SAT ALONE in his study which had been furnished with nautical wall hangings and had resembled the Captain's quarters that he occupied during voyages aboard the Queen's vessel. This was intentional. By resting in his study, the Captain was able to revive the omnipotent authority and unwavering confidence he had obtained within that portion of his life. He couldn't grasp it again.

The Captain unhinged a dock rope that was displayed on the north wall and then returned to sit with the bulky rope lain across his lap. He twisted the rope, inspecting the strands that tightened and loosened as he moved his hands. It was old rope the Captain had carried with him ever since he had retired from sailing years ago. He wrapped the rope around his neck and pulled it tight enough to choke. Satisfied, the Captain tied the rope into a noose and placed it on the chair's side. He had a rocks glass with brandy on the end table and took it with him when he left.

He found Margot writing letters in the library. They were addressed to the families of the victims at her ball. Delamar leaned against the back of her chair.

"You are not to see Daniel again."

Her hand stopped mid word. She sat frozen as her husband made his way to the other end of the library.

"The way you act," Margot hissed.

Delamar was at the table in an instant and slammed his open palm against the table.

"I still see that whore when I look at him!" Margot screamed.

"Shut your mouth!" the Captain ordered. He cocked back an open palm while his other hand clenched the neat glass of bourbon. Margot flinched and held herself there, expecting the blow at any moment. A violent shaking rattled the Captain, and suddenly the glass shattered in his hand. The bourbon splashed into the fresh cuts making Delamar clench his teeth.

He used tweezers to pull the pieces of glass from his hand then washed it clean with water and alcohol. Delamar opened the door to the basement and walked down the steps. Daniel was awake with his head bent back resting on the stone wall. The Captain searched Daniel's face, looking closely at his features, and then he sighed.

"You resemble her," the Captain said with disgust.

"My mother was beautiful. I look like a monster."

"She was beautiful," the Captain agreed. "Daniel, I know you are troubled. I know something has twisted your thoughts. I know that you have chosen to forget everything that happened. And now, you have killed so many people. You are sick. I am sorry, but we must hang you for what you have done."

"You have a debt. They all had a debt."

"Do you remember how you escaped?"

Daniel thought for some time. He remembered walking in the desert; for a long time, he walked in the desert thirsty and tired and hot, too hot. "I walked out."

"Yes. But how?"

Daniel's head hurt, as if trying to dig up the memory was ripping out parts of his brain and throwing them to the side to find what was underneath. The Captain standing outside the cage, the desert, the heat which had melted into his brain, he remembered these.

"You have chosen to forget," the Captain decided.

"Not what you've done."

"I only ever tried to help, Daniel."

"My mother actually loved you. I bet that got you stiff thinking about how you had her in your palm and could do whatever you wanted with her for your pleasure."

"Daniel, I loved her."

Daniel roared, "Shut up! Shut the hell up! Liar!" He was on his feet flinging his arms about, scrambling back and forth in the confined space like a beast.

The Captain neared the bars and shouted. "You lost your goddamn mind, Daniel. You're my biggest mistake, and your mother would have been better off—alive, even—if you weren't such a child."

Daniel's hand was around the Captain's neck at an instant. Delamar tried to pry his neck free as Daniel squeezed his thumb deep into the Captain's windpipe.

"I'll take what you owe!"

Delamar planted the top of his feet against the bars and pushed back, but Daniel held tight. He got his other hand around the Captain's neck then dug in both thumbs, sealing off his breathing. The Captain scratched at Daniel's hands then went to punch him, but Daniel pulled the Captain's face in and bashed his head against the bars. Daniel did this again and again, whipping Delmar's head back farther each time as blood splashed against the bars and splattered onto Daniel's face. The Captain brought his forearm up to protect his head from another blow, but Daniel tightened his grip and the Captain's skin turned purple. The Captain's body began to go limp. His legs gave way, the weight of his head was too much for his neck. Keeping his eyes open was an impossibility.

Suddenly Daniel's hands opened, and he fled to the corner of the cage as a bullet sparked against the bars. Margot stood with a six-round revolver and fired again, but this shot struck the bars as well.

The Captain motioned Margot to put her gun down before a deathly shake came over him, and then he passed out there on his side. Margot looked up at Daniel and then told him, "You need to hang."

She pulled the Captain from the cage then brought her ear to his mouth and listened. She watched his chest, hoping for it to regulate. His forehead was pushed in about a tenth an inch and blood was clumping out unevenly. Margot wiped sweat from her forehead and fanned herself as she tried to catch her breath. She pulled at her hair with her fingers. "Joseph!" she screamed. "Fuck!" In her panic she began pacing the room with no direction. "I need the doctor, Ryan! Where is Ryan?" She asked aloud to herself.

Daniel laughed.

"What's so goddamn funny, you freak!"

"The Captain will see Ryan soon enough." Daniel rested his head back against the wall with a cocked grin.

"And he'll fix him right up!"

Daniel chuckled. "Right."

"What's the fucking joke?"

"I shot the doctor. Andrew Ryan is dead." Daniel stared at the ceiling as his smile stretched across his potted cheeks.

"I'll call for the doctor in the next town!"

"Captain's already half dead."

Margot bolted up the stairs and ran out of the house. Daniel composed himself and studied the Captain.

"Always thought this was my grave."

———

THE HOSPITAL HAD TWO columns of eight beds, each lined along the walls with a pathway between the two that was wide enough for one person to walk through at a time. A nurse was sweeping dirt off the adobe floor when the Marshal woke. She walked to him, and he tried to speak, but the nurse told him to save his strength for the doctor. Then she brought a tin of water to his lips. As O'Hara shifted, a throbbing sensation made him flinch, letting some water spill onto his scarred shoulder. He pulled his shirt up and looked at his stomach where the metal bar had previously been stuck in him. It was gone, and the wound was stitched closed. The stitching was messy, with loose thread hanging in spots and skin being forced in crude, uneven ways to a close.

The nurse glanced at the shoddy work before commenting, "Soon as the doctor gets here he will have that done properly."

"Did you do this?" the Marshal asked with a clueless air.

The nurse smirked. "I sure hope not. A man left you on the doorstep with that masterpiece."

The nurse ground aloe vera in a bowl and mixed it with a cup of diluted alcohol till it became a green mush and then applied it to the Marshal's burnt back. O'Hara tried not to jolt despite the throbbing he felt as she generously lathered the remedy.

Finally, the doctor came in and introduced himself to the Marshal before promptly shoving a rag into O'Hara's mouth. The doctor then cut open O'Hara's stitches and began. O'Hara bit into the rag, screaming as his wound opened wide and blood gushed out.

"Hold still," the doctor ordered.

A man ran to the bedside, panting as the nurse chased behind him. She yelled, "He is in surgery, you're going to have to wait!"

"Doctor! We need you in Delamar. The Captain himself is half dead!" he urged.

The Doctor, keeping his eyes on O'Hara's wound, replied, "If I stop, he will die."

"There's no time!"

"What do you suggest?"

"How much money do you want? Delamar will pay it! The Captain's life is worth more than this guy's!"

O'Hara shot a stern look at the man, then turned to see the doctor's reaction.

"He's a U.S. Marshal."

"Okay, take him with you. I'll drive, and you can fix him up in the back."

"You want me to move, then stitch up, a U.S. Marshal in the back of a bouncing Model T?

"The Captain is gonna die!"

After pulling another stitch through, the doctor gave in and asked for the man's help to haul O'Hara into the back of the motor vehicle. The Marshal had lost all the color in his face, let alone a sizable portion of the blood. The engine turned over and the man drove frantically toward Delamar, not minding any bumps in the road. The doctor and the Marshal bounced in the backseat, causing the doctor to stab O'Hara with the needle multiple times. O'Hara's sweat seeped into the seat causing it to feel spongy. His eyes closed. "Keep your eyes open! Stay with me, dammit! Christ!" the doctor shouted as he shook the Marshal, but it was no use. O'Hara faded into sleep.

23 ½

THE MORNING SUNLIGHT beamed through the wind-shield, and when it struck the Marshal he roused awake. He was lying curled in the fetal position before. As he shifted up to his side, the blood-soaked seat squished noisily. It took O'Hara five minutes or so to pull himself upright, and when he did, he felt the tight stitching on his stomach. The area around the stitching was bruised and swollen, but it wasn't all too painful for the look of it. O'Hara poked the inflamed area, which had become numb and stiff, then tucked his shirt into his pant line. There was a tin container designed to fit in a suit pocket that was laying on the floor of the vehicle. Samuel took up the tin and read the morphine label. He swallowed two pills and put the tin in his pocket before he eased over to the passenger door. He climbed out the Model T which was parked outside a grand manor. An eerie, distant scream came from the mansion. The front door was open wide and swaying in the wind as if the house had been broken into. O'Hara limped to the door and peered inside. The scream was vibrant, but unintelligible. It was a man's scream. O'Hara checked to his left and right as he entered the manor, wary of a possible attack. The interior was decorated with lavish art and its architecture had been inspired by English design. O'Hara was of the opinion that it was over-ly formal. That the rooms were so clean and the furnishings so pristine it didn't allow leisure or a sense of ease like a home ought to. The pocket revolver that O'Hara had when he con-fronted Jesse yesterday at the site of the train's derailment was still in his tattered and burnt suit jacket. The Iver Johnson had three rounds in the five chambers and the Marshal wondered how many wishbones he must had pulled apart throughout his life to have this kind of luck, not to mention how fortunate he was to even have the gun on him after all of yesterday's events. He followed the screaming to a door tucked out of sight near the back of the house where the stairs twisted down a murky path. All the grand décor disappeared. Only cement stair and stone ceiling remained. As the Marshal descended, the air become stale and the screaming echoed along the concrete walls. At the bottom of the stairs, Daniel was grinning as he watched the Captain's agony. The doctor repositioned the torn skin on the Captain's forehead so it would be ready to stitch properly and then began. Samuel went unnoticed. The doctor urged the Captain to be still as the Captain wailed in pain, and Daniel hollered. Finally, Daniel saw the Marshal on the stair.

"Lawman?" Daniel asked.

O'Hara raised his gun. "What is this?"

"His slow march toward death," Daniel smiled.

O'Hara watched the Captain faintly control his breathing. "He ain't gonna die."

"He will." Daniel nodded.

"Not today."

"Today. Here." Daniel patted a spot on the floor in the cell with his foot as if to mark the exact spot where the Captain would die.

The doctor had the last piece of hanging skin clenched in his tongs and brought it up carefully and sewed it to the proper spot. He then wrapped the Captain's head in a thick white bandage before telling the Captain, in a coaxing tone, that they would move him to a bed for rest. The Captain disagreed, and between grunts ordered the doctor out, which he begrudgingly obeyed. The Marshal took the morphine tin from his pocket and tossed it beside the Captain. The Captain reached for the tin and swallowed three pills then sat up with his back to the wall and studied the lawman.

"So, you're the law dog," the Captain said staunchly.

O'Hara unveiled his badge.

"U.S. Marshal." The Captain acted if he were impressed.

"Not many people have a prison in their basement."

"It has its use."

"Pretty regular," Daniel broke in.

"He's a criminal. Keeping him prisoner is like a tree growing in the forest or a boat being out on the water. It is the intended way of the world," Delamar reasoned.

"I'd feel more comfortable if it was legal," the Marshal addressed the Captain.

"No, he hangs an hour after noon today. The last of the Delamar survivors are holding up in the old inn across the stables. We all mean to watch him hang."

"You don't have no trial papers for a hanging."

"A trial is a privilege."

"Yeah, but that ain't the way the Constitution was wrote."

"Marshal, this is what they are owed," Daniel urged.

"How long did you have him set up here for?" the Marshal questioned.

"He's been here for about a day and a half."

"Don't go trying to have fun with me."

The Captain paused, then replied, "He was locked up for the better part of four years."

"I escaped. Delamar crumbled," Daniel pressed.

"You will hang, but after the court of Los Angeles decides so," the Marshal said, shifting his glare toward the prisoner. "Understand that, Captain?"

The Captain nodded.

"You got coffee?"

"Upstairs."

"How about me and you enjoy a warm mug?"

"Margot will freshen a pot for you, but I have to politely decline"

"It ain't optional."

"I'm a victim," the Captain responded numbly.

"Ain't we all."

The Marshal helped Delamar up and they ascended the stairway leaving Daniel behind. They came to the living room and sat across from each other and had a good look before either spoke. Margot hurried the Captain's side when she saw him sitting in the living room, then jumped when she noticed the battered Marshal. The Captain faced her and assured her that he was fine and that he needed to speak with the man alone.

"Get a tin ready, would you?"

"Forget the coffee," O'Hara ordered.

"Okay," Margot responded. "We all are getting awfully anxious about the hanging." Margot was assuming her innocent character when she said this, and despite saying it to her husband, the show was for the Marshal.

"There won't be a hanging. This Marshal here is determined on escorting Daniel to trial."

Margot turned pale. "No, we have all been waiting for a hanging."

"Tough."

"We ain't going to accept that. I ain't going to accept that."

"Go tell the rest, and I don't want to hear nothing more about it."

Margot stood thinking for a few seconds before discreetly moving to the back door and stepping outside.

"Who was on that train?" The Marshal asked, breaking the silence that had set.

"The survivors of Delamar were on that train."

"I don't want a damn story, Captain."

The Captain paused. "There is no use in questioning me if you have decided I'm a liar."

"No one decided anything."

"There is malice in you, Marshal. You are striking my accounts before I can relay them."

"I got a picture, and the things you are accounting for are strongly against that picture."

"Humor me."

"Three men on that train were in a shootout. I was one of em. So was your guest." The Marshal pointed down toward the basement cell. "Thing is, my part of the train had some difficulties, and I had to take an early stop. I came real close to dying, and if I'm telling the truth, I still feel near death. But I walked on and found the train on its side because the tracks had been pried out. I didn't think much on it then. I was preoccupied. See, Daniel was in the train, so he couldn't have pulled apart the tracks. And even then, that is a tall order for one man. The only other character in this case is you. So you went ahead of the train with the Delamar men you had rescued from the ball and tore up those tracks. And when the train fell, you picked Daniel up from it and brought him here. A trap clever enough to catch a fox. Thing is, you had to fill that train with people. So who were those people that were effectively your bait? Innocent people. I know. Kids, families, random people that you let on that train."

"Daniel needed to be stopped. You had no grip on it. How many people had already died? I had to resolve this. So I survived."

"No, those people didn't have any association. You could have had Delamar people on the train. Least they knew what was coming. Had a part in this."

"I didn't think of that; counterproductive to put them where Daniel would want them."

"No. You thought it. And you knew it would mean Daniel would kill more Delamar men, get back at you a little more. Truth is, you were tired of losing."

The Captain averted his eyes.

"I don't much give a shit about the past. About what horror you put that boy through. He put you through horror, eye for an eye. And if that train was filled with the people it should have been filled with, hell, we might have actually had a good time drinking coffee. You used blood you didn't own. That ain't ever gonna sit with me."

Delamar thought about what the Marshal said, past the throbbing in his skull from pain and anger.

"I owe nothing." The Captain stood.

"You want to run that again?"

"I owe nothing to you or anyone, Marshal."

The Marshal's eyes narrowed like a hawk's.

"A man should not be prosecuted for protecting his family. I won't abide, Marshal."

"That's not what you did, and that's not your decision."

"And what do you intend to do if I do not—"

The Marshal had his gun out and the barrel raised to the gauze wrapped around Delamar's skull before he could finish.

"Don't use your tongue that way with me, Captain." O'Hara pressed the steel nose against the wound. The Captain folded in agony, falling to the couch.

"I tried everything to help that boy!" the Captain started defensively. "Years of trying to make things right for him."

"I already told you I don't give a shit about the past."

"I thought of Daniel like a son."

"Sure got a nice room for him."

"Marshal, I had to take care of Daniel. What he became is my responsibility."

"The law is not."

"The boy, he killed his mother. And it destroyed him. He was guilty, and the town voted him guilty, but even though he was guilty, I... I didn't have the skin for it. The night before he was set to hang, I unlocked the cell and told him to run west. I know he lost a good part of his mind in that cell, because of Margot. She took out her fire on him. But what parts of his mind he still had, the desert took. All of this, Marshal, is my mess. It's why I didn't wait for the law. It's why he was meant to hang today. I wanted to clear my mistake."

"So your wife did that to Daniel?"

"Daniel told her what me and his mother were doing. She knew better than to reproach me about it. I came back one day and found him the way he was. I extended the hanging date four times. I couldn't decide if what my wife did earned him a pass."

"He killed his own ma?"

The Captain nodded. "I was there."

"Why?"

"He found out what me and his mother were doing, then took up his late father's gun and shot his mother."

"Was she more than just a good time for you?"

"She was. Margot knew that."

―――――――――――

DURING THE HEAT OF the Marshal's and the Captain's discussion, Margot snuck into the house using the back door with rope and the six-chambered revolver that was still in her pocket from earlier. She crept down the staircase to Daniel and saw him sitting in his usual corner of the cell. Daniel watched her move the wooden chair to the middle of the room and then stand on it. She flung the rope over a ceiling beam and tied it there. She measured the rope to her neck's height, then raised it a few inches and began to fashion the hangman's knot.

After two attempts, she had the noose where she wanted it, and then stepped off the chair and moved over to the cell gate. She had the revolver out as she slid the key into the lock and opened the cell, then walked back a distance.

"Come on." She gestured at Daniel with the barrel.

Daniel stood slowly, but stayed in the corner.

"Hurry up," Margot hissed.

Daniel stepped through the opening and made his way to the face of the chair and looked up at the noose.

"Go on," Margot urged.

"It ain't tied right," Daniel mumbled as he continued to stare at the rope.

Margot glanced up at the knot, and Daniel took the chair in his hand and swung it at Margot. She brought the revolver forward to fire, but the leg of the chair struck the back of her hand and the revolver clattered to the floor. Daniel grabbed it and brought the hilt of the piece to Margot's temple, knocking her out before she could scream.

WHEN A RALLY OF BULLETS fired in the distance, the Marshal and the Captain stood up. Another succession of shots sounded, and they were sure it was coming from the saloon. O'Hara was positioned at the door with his ear against the wood as he eased it open far enough for a visual.

"It's Daniel," O'Hara stated.

"See him?"

"No, I hear it. That's what's worse." Gunshots echoed through the empty terrain. Delamar confirmed O'Hara's suspicion when he found Margot slumped on the cell floor.

"Grab a gun and trench yourselves in a tight spot, I'm going on after him," the Marshal called down the stairs.

"Hold up, Marshal," Delamar called back.

"He will be mighty pleased if I brought you with me."

"This is my mess, Marshal."

O'Hara grimaced before making his way out and across the wooden porch and behind the Model T where he crouched against the sheet metal. The Captain followed him with a scoped rifle clutched at chest height.

It was noon when the two came around the back side of the saloon. The Marshal realized that there hadn't been any shots since they had left the Captain's manor, which could mean that Daniel was bunkered in the saloon, waiting. The Marshal counted three holes in the wall that had been bored through during the racket. He hugged the wall as he made his way to a window and peered inside, seeing the mess of bodies, shattered glassware, and splintered wood. O'Hara pressed his ear to the wall and listened with his mouth hung slightly open and his eyes shut. There was nothing to hear. Delamar pointed at the house then mouthed the words, "Is he there?" Samuel didn't have an answer.

At different intervals, O'Hara traded between glancing through the window and listening intently as he considered the different options Daniel had and which one he would take. Samuel checked on the Captain, who was lying on his stomach behind a collection of tumbleweed thicket. He peered through the scope, scanning the perimeter, and was ready to fire.

The Marshal decided what he was to do. He rounded the corner, keeping his shoulder against the wood as he made his way to the saloon porch. He removed his boots and walked soundlessly to the double swinging doors that were hinged to the door panel. The Marshal shoved the doors open then hunkered behind the wall, but it didn't cause anything to happen. He waited for the doors to settle before he pushed past them and into the saloon. Blood was still flowing out of some of the men, but none had any life left. Some had managed to get their guns in hand before being shot down. He shook a revolver out of one man's hand and checked the chamber. It was full—not even a chance to fire back, the Marshal realized before tucking the revolver under his belt. O'Hara navigating around the broken glass and human innards by choosing his steps carefully. He figured Daniel wasn't positioned anywhere in the saloon, but O'Hara didn't want to throw the dice. After he was satisfied, O'Hara called out for the Captain to come in.

The scene looked like any other instance of Daniel's work that the Marshal had investigated before it. Men were slaughtered. O'Hara counted twenty-two of them and twenty-five shots, one in each body, save for the three that had had cut through the far wall. "That's new," O'Hara thought, comparing the absolute precision Daniel had in the church and on the Higgans' ranch. Delamar came through the doors with his rifle slung on his back and the Marshal's boots in hand. He stared at the massacre.

"The usual," O'Hara stated.

The Captain let the boots fall to the floor where O'Hara picked them up and put them on.

"At the ball, I gathered what I could out of the confusion. Got the people nearest the band and led them out the back through the stage and the servant's quarters. They followed me, entrusting their selves to me. And I brought them here." the Captain said.

"You and me aren't so skilled at saving lives, I guess. The rate and the nature of this case leads me to believe that I ain't going to save a single soul."

"I hope you're adept at killing, Marshal," the Captain said before positioning his rifle along the shattered window frame.

There was a blast. For an instant, O'Hara considered that the Captain had fired a round, but he knew it was too far off to be the Captain. It came from the Delamar Manor.

2

———

DANIEL LEFT THE DOOR open as he stepped into the Delamar manor. Margot froze when she saw him; she was holding a damp rag to her temple which had been bleeding from the pistol whipping that Daniel had given her in the basement. Her stare fell to the pocket gun that Daniel had positioned at his hip.

"All 700 voted," Daniel spoke. "700 will die."

"The women, you know we weren't allowed to vote." Margot blurted out defensively.

"Those 699 gentlemen voted me guilty, they damned me."

Daniel came face to face with Margot and removed the rag from her bloody forehead. He dug the barrel's nose into her abdomen, and she winced.

"I set out to collect the debt of 700 gentlemen."

"Please, don't." Margot turned away, but Daniel gripped her chin and yanked it back.

"Look."

She did. His face was a hideous contortion of demonic skin at this intimate distance.

"I forgave one debt—look at me!" He pinned her head to the wall and went on letting his spit spray onto her face. "So I'll settle my debt, with 699 gentlemen, and one bitch."

And he shot her through the thick of her body where the bullet bored into her chest and nested in her spine. Margot collapsed to the floor, but her eyes stayed on Daniel. He watched her eyes fade till he was satisfied.

Daniel found a coach gun in an open safe upstairs and loaded it before he hid in the corner behind the front door and waited. The Captain ran in first, but Daniel waited till the Marshal came through before acting. O'Hara had his sights lined up and panned the room for Daniel, but, unfortunately, he started on his left. Daniel led the steel barrel of the pocket gun to ease up against the side of the Marshal's head; the Marshal grimaced when he felt it. The Captain was shaking Margot before he noticed Daniel, who had the coach lined with the Captain's face and the revolver aimed at the square of the Marshal's back. The Captain stood cautiously with his arms on his head and traded a glance with O'Hara. They paced to the basement entrance when Daniel beckoned them inside with a gesture of his head. The two trudged down the steps with each of their hands folded behind their backs as Daniel followed them from a few steps up.

When they reached the basement, Daniel ordered the Marshal into the cell, and he obeyed. Daniel then told the Captain to place the chair under the hangman's knot that had been fashioned earlier, and he did.

"Go on," Daniel said.

The Captain stepped up and got the round of the rope between his hands and held it there for a moment.

"You gonna make me watch this?" O'Hara asked from behind the cell bars.

"Teach you bout the law, lawman," Daniel affirmed.

"Even to this point, you deny your fault," Delamar said.

"Did you kill your own mother?" O'Hara questioned. "Delemar said you did. I have a tough time swallowing that."

The Captain glared at the Marshal.

"He owes me a debt. This is the grave of Delamar, and I mean to see a hanging."

"I'm not guilty. I will not hang myself. I will not feed into your tantrum. You killed your mother! You are a fucked child!" the Captain shouted in accusation.

"Wear that rope!" Daniel roared.

"You have chosen to forget. Remember the night, Daniel."

———————

RAIN PELTED THE CLAY desert and lightning bolts lit the night, which were followed by the cracking sounds that seemed to shake the sky. A hammering against the door flooded the house with such a presence it could be felt in each room. Dora shifted in the rocking chair and placed her book on the end table beside her. A second volley of hammering vibrated through the walls of the house.

"Danny!" Dora called.

Daniel marched half asleep to the top of the second-story stairs and rubbed his waking eyes. He jumped at the banging sound when it came the third time. Then he retrieved his late father's revolver from its beveled case which was set atop a nightstand.

Dora anxiously came to the door and was surprised when she saw Captain Delamar on the other side of the window in a suit that was caked in mud.

"What are you doing?" she asked, letting him in. Delamar flung his coat to the floor and pressed Dora against his chest. His lips sucked playfully on her neck, and the stench of alcohol that lingered on his saliva rose up to her.

She pushed back. "What is this?"

Delamar slid his arms around her waist and pressed his hips to hers. Dora dug her elbows between his forearms and pushed them off her. She fled back into the kitchen where the candles had been put out hours ago, making a point of facing the Captain while she did.

"Are you not glad to see me?" the Captain slurred.

"I'm glad, but this is not," Dora whispered back, stopping to slap Delamar's hand away. "Daniel is here."

"He's asleep," the Captain dismissed as he brought his hands to Dora's shoulders and massaged them tenderly with the tips of his fingers.

"Not with the racket you made. You're drunk," Dora hissed.

Delamar fitted his fingers under the shoulder seams of Dora's blouse and rubbed the warm skin underneath. "Stop!" Dora yelled in his ear as he held her against the kitchen wall in the pitch-black room. The Captain groped the base of Dora's neck then felt down under the bust of the dress, ripping the shoulder off and leaving Dora exposed. She shoved him away, shouting, "Get off me!"

In the hall, Daniel stood with a candle lit in the chamberstick and the revolver in his other hand pointed at the man who was forcing himself on his mother. When Dora pushed the Captain away from her, Daniel took advantage of the distance between her and the attacker by raising the gun and cocking the revolver's hammer back.

"Daniel, no!" Dora shouted.

The Captain turned to see Daniel with the gun aimed at his chest. Daniel shut his eyes before he fired, and Delamar raised his hands to try to fend off the blast. The shot broke through the house as if the home had been torn apart by the roar of thunder. Daniel was scared to open his eyes, but when he did, he saw his mother standing in front of the Captain with blood seeping out and staining the tattered dress. Daniel rushed to her in tears, letting the candle and gun clatter to the floor.

"Mom! Mom!" Daniel called as his tears blinded him. He faced the Captain, "You owe me! She didn't deserve this!"

"Daniel, you..." the Captain muttered, unable to finish.

"I WON'T," THE CAPTAIN said as he let the hangman's knot swing away.

"It's your fault she died," Daniel shouted as he thumbed the hammer back. He had the coach gun addressing O'Hara all the while. O'Hara shifted, aligning himself with Daniel.

"Move again, give me a reason." Daniel threatened the Marshal by stroking the shotgun's trigger.

O'Hara hesitated. Daniel would be able to fire that coach before O'Hara could even get his gun out from under his belt, and missing wasn't really a thing with pellet fire at that distance. But the cell bars were solid enough to ricochet any shot that hit. There was a slim possibility that no pellets would hit him, but even more that the determined pellets that passed through the bars wouldn't kill him. As long as he wasn't cleaned out by that first shot, he could line the revolver between the bars and end it. But that all seemed mighty hopeful compared to likely scenario of taking pellets to the gut and dying here in this cell.

The Captain's face pleaded to the Marshal.

"No, you're out of luck, Captain. This Marshal don't like putting his life up. He didn't in Los Angeles; he won't here," Daniel said.

When O'Hara looked away from the Captain, Delamar cursed him.

"Fact is, in that city of angels, you gave me a reason to keep on living. I owe you that, law dog."

"Just do it," the Captain groaned.

"You accept, then?"

"I won't, not even at gunpoint. Just do it."

"That would be the gentleman thing to do."

"Fuck you!" Delamar cursed, shutting his eyes.

O'Hara snatched the revolver from his pant line, and when Daniel saw he fired both the revolver and shotgun simultaneously. The bullet flung the Captain from the chair after landing between his eyes. Sparks burst out from the cell bars, and the Marshal was forced back by two pellets that snagged his hip, but he kept on his feet, lined the shot, and fired. The bullet tore into Daniel's shoulder and spun him with such an immense enough force that his grip failed, letting the guns drop as his feet gave way. O'Hara limped over to Daniel, who was unable to reach the revolver because of damage to his shoulder. The Marshal came near him and struck Daniel with the hilt of the Iver Johnson, knocking Daniel unconscious. O'Hara flipped

Daniel's body over and cuffed him, then sat on the staircase. His hip was messy, but it wasn't fatal. More like a bad graze.

Chunks of skull and brain pooled in the spill of blood that had collected from the back end of the Captain's head. After shutting Delamar's eyes, O'Hara pained his way up the stairs to wash his wounds.

IT WAS SOMEWHERE NOT far off a shoddy wagon road in the Nevada desert where the Marshal parked the Model T. He walked over to the back door of the car, and opened it for Daniel, whose hands were cuffed behind his back. Daniel stumbled out and O'Hara tied a rope to the chain linking Daniel's cuffs, then fastened the other end round the car's tire.

O'Hara looked at Daniel then gestured to nearby shrubbery.

Daniel paced to the spot and weaved through the shrubs till he came to a drop-off that was hugged by a river bank. He climbed down to stand along the meager river that was a dying stream trickling between desert pebbles. Here, the rope pulled, and Daniel could move no further.

O'Hara leaned on the side of the car where sunlight heated the back of his neck as he panned the vast idleness laid out before him. He thought it looked plenty nice.

A gunshot fired and woke the desert with its cry. O'Hara started up and saw the rope's slack fall. He drew his revolver and followed the rope trail hurriedly, keeping his firing stance as he did.

When he came over the shrubs, he saw Daniel laid out on the river bank. There wasn't any life in him; his torso had been blasted through by pellet shot. O'Hara studied Daniel before searching the area for anything. He didn't have a clue of what he was looking for, but he found something nonetheless—it was a shotgun shell. It was there in the stream, and it was shining from the harsh sunlight when O'Hara picked it up and brought it to his face. The Marshal knew what was on the other side of that shell, so he just tossed it back to the stream.

———————

NOW I HAVE REALIZED that there ain't much point in writing you with me already on my way back and all. Hell, I'll see you before this letter does, most likely, but I got things I want to write, and you're always good enough to look through em.

The papers are going to get real excited about this, and all the tall tales will be spread in that ink. I ain't gonna waste my time with em, and I think that's a good practice to follow. I'll just wait for it to be all forgot, for the truth to come to em. Then I'll read it. See, the admirable thing about the truth is that when it sets in, it stays. Nothing's gonna change that.

Looking back at the whole deal, I don't know if me being a part did anything. No one was saved. And I ain't harassing myself in that regard, and I ain't trying to feel bad for myself, neither. I'm just really thinking about that. My heart ain't bothered by it, but my mind keeps asking, and if I sat and honestly told myself what I believe, it's that no, I couldn't had changed anything.

Don't be afraid to tell me no, but I was thinking about the baby and what to call it and thought of some other names instead. Like I said, it's a suggestion, no disrespect to your mother. Victoria, Tori O'Hara, and George O'Hara are fine sounding names. But what if instead we named em Reed or Elizabeth?

-Samuel O'Hara

1

Don't miss out!

Click the button below and you can sign up to receive emails whenever Elijah Cooksey publishes a new book. There's no charge and no obligation.

https://books2read.com/r/B-A-KQVE-HOYQ

Connecting independent readers to independent writers.

About the Author

Elijah Cooksey is a no frills writer who crafts his stories to be as efficient as possible. He takes pride in his concise approach. His early work consists of multiple scripts, most notably Warborn, which is planned to be converted into a trilogy by himself.Mr. Cooksey's latest release is a grim western novel and is dense with gun slinging action and sparse on dialogue. 700 Gentlemen is the opening story of the "Dead West" series. Expect the second entry in 2020.At the moment, his second novel, Play, is set to be released at the end of the fourth quarter of 2018. His brother, Samuel Cooksey, is also a writer. He released Hayley and The Beserker King.